Weddings& Wands

A Paranormal Witch Cozy Mystery

Book Store Cozy Mystery Series
Book 12

Lucinda Race

MC Two Press

Editor NN Light Editing Services
Cover design by Mariah Sinclair

Manufactured in the United States of America
First Edition May 2025

Print Edition ISBN 978-1-966424-12-3
E-book ISBN 978-1-966424-11-6

Pembroke Cove, ME
CAFE
1
2
3
4
5
6
7
8
9
10
11
12
13
14
Doenut Drive
Main Street
Route 1
Park Square
MOTEL
1. Robin's Cafe
2. Bygone Antiques
3. The Pembroke Cliffs
4. Cozy Nook Bookstore
5. Twisted Scissors Hair Salon
6. Betty's Market
7. Old Town Library
8. Miss Judy's Dance Studio
9. The Sweet Spot Baker
10. Bee Bee's Boutique
11. Tuckers Hardware Store
12. The Copper Kettle
13. Police Station
14. Town Hall

Chapter 1
Lily

* * *

Nikki entered the kitchen and discovered me sitting with a brown paper bag cupped in my hands, blowing into it. Milo's paw was on my shoulder. "Breathe in. Breathe out."

She dropped to her knees. "Lily, what's wrong?"

I gazed into her worried eyes. "The wedding is in less than a week." I thrust a scroll of paper in her direction. "Just look at this."

It trailed from her hands to the floor. She looked at me, her eyes wide. "Is this your to-do list?"

I nodded and blew into the bag again.

She snapped her fingers and, holding a fragrant cup of chamomile tea, slipped an arm around my shoulders. "Drink this. It's your mom's blend."

"Nikki, it's a good thing you're here. My dear witch has been like this for half an hour."

I flashed Milo a grateful smile. "And my handsome familiar hasn't left my side."

She eased the bag from my fingers. "You have an army of people ready to help you prepare for the wedding." Scanning the list, she said, "I'm going to call our moms and pass off most of this to them. They'll be thrilled to help. Your aunt has the bookstore covered, so we're free today to drive into Drakes Bay and pick up our dresses."

"Maybe we should fly. We'd get there quicker."

With a shake of her head, Nikki pulled me to my feet. "Not a chance. We're going to stop for lunch and enjoy our girls' day." Giving me a little push toward my bedroom, she gave me a pointed look. "Get dressed while I make some calls."

"How come your wedding was so much easier to organize?"

She laughed. "How quickly you forget. A murderer destroyed my gown, treasure hunters were dressed as leprechauns, and a dead man was in my bathtub at the inn. It was anything but a breeze, but you took care of everything just like I'm going to do for you."

Milo said, "You can start by feeding me breakfast before I starve."

Instead of going down the hall, I whirled

around and kissed him on the head. "Coming right up."

Nikki twirled me around. "I'll take care of Milo. Now go."

I saw the rerolled scroll sitting on the table; her smile couldn't mask the steely glint in her eyes that told me I didn't have a choice.

She pointed to my room. "Go. Today's going to be so much fun."

I gave her a quick hug. "You're right. It's a perfect August morning, and I'm marrying the most amazing man in six days."

The back door opened, and my handsome fiancé strode in. Gage held a bouquet of wildflowers. "Hello there." His eyebrows wiggled, and mischief hovered in his eyes. "I thought you ladies would be almost out the door by now."

Milo yawned. "We would have been if a certain witch hadn't melted down before breakfast."

Gage glanced at Nikki. "Care to translate?"

As a non-magical, Gage couldn't understand familiar speak. I scooped Milo up. "All he said was we're running late. I'll be right back."

Leaving Nikki and Gage, I carried him down the hall and whispered in his ear, "I didn't have a total meltdown, just normal bride stuff."

He tapped my cheek. "If you say so, but in all the years we've lived together, that was the first, and hopefully last, time I saw you blowing into a bag. You don't do that when you find a dead body. *What* is it about weddings that make people get so uptight?"

"I'm worried that everything won't be perfect. I've waited a long time to marry Gage and for us to live under the same roof as a family."

I felt Milo's body relax. "Perfection is overrated, and it won't matter what happens if the ice melts too fast or we run out of food." He held up a paw. "Which we won't; we have too many witches at the reception for anything to go wrong. In the end, all that matters is you and Detective Cutie. And, of course, the most important familiar at the event."

I chuckled. My heart was lighter than it had been just moments ago. "I love you, Milo."

He wriggled from my arms and dropped to the floor. "Don't get all mushy on me." He stalked from the room. I wrapped my arms around my waist and sighed. How that little gray fur ball took away my worries with a few sentences was beyond me, but he was the best familiar a witch could have.

I dashed through the shower, slipping into cropped linen slacks and a pale pink sweater set. Not bad. I tousled my short, sun-streaked hair. Since it was a girls' day, I added a swish of mascara, a quick flick of blush, and bronze eyeshadow. Now, I felt more like a bride-to-be.

When I entered the kitchen, Gage stopped talking, his mouth slightly agape. He crossed the room in three long strides and took my hands, leaning in to kiss my cheek. "You're beautiful."

I felt the blush creep up my neck to my hairline. "Thank you."

Milo was perched on a chair eating breakfast and Nikki sat at the table.

She grinned. "Now you look like you're ready for an adventure. Gage, we're going to shop until we drop."

He kissed my lips. "Steve and I are moving some of my stuff over today. I thought it'd be good timing with you and Nikki out and about. Also, I'll wait for the living room furniture delivery this morning. Any specific instructions?"

I placed my hands on his cheeks and pulled his face to mine. "This is your home, too. Arrange everything as you want, and if I don't like it, we'll chat later, but I'm sure it will be perfect, just like our future."

He chuckled. "I'm not sure if perfect is the best word, but our life won't be dull."

"You two should settle for no murders before the wedding and call that perfection."

I laughed. "We have had our share, and nothing will mar our special day." Giving Gage a quick kiss, I said, "Ready to hit the road, Nik?"

Milo stretched out. "I'm going to stay here and supervise."

Gage grinned when Milo grumbled and lay down. "I have a boss?"

"More like a guard." My fingers trailed down his rugged jawline. A shiver of concern raced down my spine. "Be careful today." I held up my hand. "Wait there." I hurried down the hall into my office and spied the velvet pouch on the desk. I picked it up, kissed it, and softly said, "Protect this man that I love from the moment our hands fit like a glove. This is my wish on behalf of our family, by blood or by choice, and so it shall be."

I walked into the kitchen and glanced at Milo, who stood beside Nikki. He nodded solemnly. It wasn't my imagination. He felt it, too. "Gage," I took his hands and clasped them together like a glove with mine. "I was going to give you this on our wedding day, but why wait?" I handed him the white velvet bag and pictured him inside a protective orb of white. Before he untied the strands, I pressed my forehead to his. "Wear this at all times. It will protect and guide you."

His eyes met mine as he studied me. "What's worrying you?"

I shook my head. "Nothing specific, just promise me."

The amulet slid into the palm of his hand, and his brow furrowed. "Isn't red for love?"

I slipped the chain over his head and placed my hand on the platinum disc and inlaid stone over his heart. "Red Jasper is a stone known for energy and endurance and has long been a talisman for warriors. But it also represents a promoter of justice, protection, and life. This amulet will give you added strength and courage."

Milo and Nikki were silent.

"You've named most of what I already stand for." His voice was gentle, as if I needed to be reminded that he represented all good and noble things in this life.

"That's true. Just as I wear a necklace to enhance my protection, by giving this to you as a testament of my love, which is the strongest magic in the universe, it'll give you protection—and me, peace of mind." I tipped my head back and saw love and absolute trust in his eyes.

"Until my last breath, I will wear this amulet." He kissed me. "Thank you."

Milo grumbled. "Now he's even more a part of the family, and it's still not official for six days."

Nikki shushed him. "Did you need a ceremony to be a part of the family?"

"No. I have Michaels blood in my veins." He swished his tail. "Besides, remember, she chose me."

"Just as she and Gage chose each other." Nikki ran a hand down Milo's back. "She needed to do this today."

He slunk across the room and ribboned around my legs. "Lily, don't worry. I'll keep an eye on things around here." With a quick scoop, I kissed him on the top of his head between his ears. He twitched them and gave me the Yoda look, the all-knowing character from Star Wars.

Gage wrapped his arms around both of us. "I'll look after things today. Have fun with Nikki." He took Milo from my arms.

"Like he can take care of witchy things." Milo huffed, leaped from Gage's arms to the floor, and stalked from the room.

"Was it something I said?" His gaze followed my familiar as he left the room.

"Don't worry about Milo. He's overly sensitive. All the changes, the construction happening, and now the wedding."

Nikki smiled behind her hand and picked up her bag. "Ready, Lily?"

Gage kissed me one more time. "Have fun, ladies."

"When I get home, remember there's no peeking in the garment bags. I'll have my dresses for the wedding."

He shut his eyes. "I've been practicing."

I kissed his cheek and held out my hand, and my bag appeared.

Nikki said, "You need to teach me that spell. I've never been able to master it."

The door opened, and I winked. "In the car." With a flutter of my fingertips over my shoulder, I blew a kiss to Gage. "See you later."

An hour later, Nikki navigated the car down Main Street in Drakes Bay, a charming oceanside town.

I pointed to the right side of the street. "Grant's Gowns is on the corner of Main and Cade Street. It's a yellow building with white shutters and black trim."

With a laugh she said, "Someone's excited. I remember where it is." She slowed the car and peered through the windshield into the bright sun. "If you see a parking space, let me know."

I was surprised to see so much activity in the town this close to the end of August. Most kids were back in school, so vacationers had thinned out. Being closer to Portland, it was a busy coastal town. "Look, someone's pulling onto the street from a spot right in front of the shop."

Nikki slid her SUV into the opening and rubbed her hands together. "I can't wait to see the dresses on you."

"I wasn't planning on trying them on again. I've had several fittings."

She shook her index finger in front of me. "Nope. You're trying them on, and I want to double check the fit on my dress, too."

"I should have called Claudia to confirm our scheduled time." I glanced at the door as the curtain fluttered.

Nikki pushed open her door. "Not to worry, I took care of that yesterday."

I wanted to say that she didn't have to do everything for me, but before I could, she grinned.

"It was on my Matron of Honor's list." She snapped her fingers and held up the scroll I showed her at my place. "Now, this is my copy, and you have almost nothing to do other than keep worry lines from your beautiful face."

With a snort, I got out of the vehicle. "Easy for you to say."

When she came around the front of the SUV, she slipped her arm through the crook of mine. "When I got married, you took care of everything. I had nothing to fret about. Let me do the same for you."

My tummy flipped when I thought of the extensive list. Then, unexpectedly, all the tension I'd been holding in my shoulders and neck evaporated. "On one condition: if you need my help, you'll ask?"

Beaming, she held the door open. "Of course." The door *whoosh*ed closed behind us. We entered a large salon where mannequins dressed in glorious gowns stood like women waiting to be asked to dance at the ball.

A young, curvaceous woman patted her long blond hair, that was tied in a blue silk ribbon that matched her eyes. She greeted us with a warm smile and extended her hands. "Lily, Nikki, I was just putting your gowns in the dressing rooms. Who's first?"

I looked at Nikki. "She is."

Claudia Grant whisked Nikki into the next

room and closed the door after them. I wandered around the soothing space, letting my fingers trail over the dress fabrics, captivated by the intricate lace work on one gown. "This is stunning."

Claudia came up behind me. "I found it in Uncle Herman's workbasket. He must have either created or purchased it and never used it. I decided it must be on a dress."

I nodded. "It's beautiful." A light breeze slid over my arm like someone brushed past me.

"Nikki's ready if you want to have a seat." She gestured to an upholstered chair.

I sat down and crossed my legs. I felt like I was being watched. When Claudia left the room, I looked around but was alone. The lacy curtains wafted from the breeze in the open window.

Claudia stepped into the room. "Here she is."

Nikki floated in and stopped, making a slow turn, swishing the skirt from side to side. "Well, what do you think?"

The sage green chiffon dress was perfect. From the sweetheart neckline to the sweep of the cascading skirt. "Nikki, you look stunning."

Her eyes were bright, and she grabbed my hand. "Put your dress on so we can stand side by side like we'll be at the altar."

I knew what she was thinking. How would our dresses look together?

Chapter 2
Lily

Claudia zipped the A-line chiffon white dress. Its sleeveless V-neck bodice was embellished with white pearls and quartz crystals to a floor-length skirt with a sweeping train. My amethyst and black tourmaline amulet was cool against my skin.

"I have the perfect pair of earrings to go with your necklace if that's what you'll wear at the wedding."

I had no intention of taking it off. "I'd love to see them."

She slipped quietly from the room as I

studied my reflection in the three-way mirror. This was the first time I truly felt like a bride. I brushed my hair into place and looked to make sure I was alone before saying a quick spell to sweep it from my face. I finished in the nick of time before Claudia returned.

"Your hair looks great like that." She handed me a pair of chandelier earrings featuring three stones. The first was a black tourmaline with two oval amethyst encased in silver filigree. I held them up to my ears and looked in the mirror. "They *do* match."

"Try them on. They can be your something borrowed."

I secured them to my ear lobes and felt a surge of energy rush through me. "Are these yours?" And more importantly, was Claudia a witch?

"They are, and I'm happy to loan them to you."

"Thank you. I'd like that, and you must come to the wedding, too. We can introduce you to our family and friends." I looked in the mirror, and she was right; they were perfect.

"Are you ready to show Nikki?"

I nodded as I wiped my cheeks dry. "Thank you, Claudia. I wasn't planning on trying on the dress, but I'm glad I did. I can't believe I'll be a bride in less than a week."

"And a beautiful one at that." She gave me a quick hug. "You still have the other dress to try on, too."

I fanned myself with a magazine. With a giggle, I said, "I'm not sure I can take the excitement."

Nikki tapped on the door. "Lily? If you're not coming out, I'm coming in."

I pulled the door open and sashayed into the main room. Holding my arms out and with a dramatic spin, I grinned. "What do you think?"

She clapped her hands together and sighed. "Oh, Lily. You were meant to be a bride. The gown is perfect. When Gage sees you, his heart's going to stop beating."

"I certainly hope not." We stood arm in arm, gazing into the mirror. "Every day of my life has led me to this point."

She nodded and sniffed. "You're meant to be together. If nothing else, the events over the last couple of years prove that."

Claudia's brow creased, but she was too polite to ask the question.

With a shrug, I said, "I've helped Gage, along with Nikki and others, solve a few murders in town."

Nikki scoffed. "A few. We've had eleven murders and, without Lily's help, some murderers might have gotten away with it."

Claudia's eyes bugged wide. "Sounds scary." She looked over her shoulder before turning back to us, her lips in a thin line. "I'm sorry. Would you excuse me for a minute?"

"Sure. I'll put the other dress on."

She hurried from the room, and I tipped my head. "Do you think she's okay?"

"I'm sure she's fine. Come on. I'll help you try on dress number two."

. . .

Nikki and I left the bridal shop carrying white garment bags over our arms. She pushed the lock on the hatch, and we laid them flat in the back. I frowned. "Do you think Claudia's all right? She seemed jumpy, don't you think?"

"Not really. She moved to Drakes Bay a couple of months ago and has poured time and energy into getting the shop ready to open. I'm sure she's excited to see three of her dresses leave the store, knowing word of mouth is the best advertisement. When people get a look at you in either of those gowns, you're her walking billboard."

I placed a hand on her arm. "You have to say that, you're my best friend. But," I looked at the tidy dress shop. "Something's not quite right in there."

"Stop looking for a mystery. You have a wedding to prepare for, and we don't have time for anything other than the rehearsal dinner, then the ceremony, and after that, it's time to party!"

I chuckled and tried to forget that hinky feeling I had a couple of times inside. Nikki was right; it was time for a celebration. "We should skip lunch and get an ice cream cone before going back to Pembroke Cove."

She shook her head. "I have a better idea. I have all the fixings to make hot fudge sundaes at my place. I'll text the guys to let them know we'll be back soon and they can meet us if they want. If not, we'll wrap up girls' day with over-flowing bowls of decadence."

When we got in the car, I relaxed. "That will hit the spot." Looking out the window as Nikki drove, we merged onto the highway. "Claudia is a talented dress designer. I hope she does well."

"Like I said, you're going to be great advertising for her business wearing two designs."

I half turned in my seat. "Nik, do you remember when you were getting married and mentioned something about other types of magical beings around Pembroke Cove?"

She nodded and glanced my way. "Why?"

"No one talks about them. Not even at coven meetings. When I tried to bring it up with Aunt Mimi, she said that when the time was right, we'd chat about them. What's the big secret?"

"No secret, exactly. We don't get along with the others. They can be," she exhaled, "challenging."

"Who are the others?" Now she had my undivided attention.

"We shouldn't be talking about this. After your wedding, Mimi was going to tell you everything."

"There's more?" My voice trailed up an octave.

She threw up one hand, and the other remained on the steering wheel. "There are three small communities nymphs, fairies, and the elementals. Fairies are more mischievous and get along with everyone, but they're shy and stick to themselves. Nymphs adore the communities they live in, but we rarely see them, as well."

"I'm going to guess the elementals aren't quite as reticent?"

"Nope."

I heard the *P* pop when Nikki answered me.

"You've gone this far; why don't you fill me in?" My insides vibrated. I wasn't sure if it was nerves or excitement but, either way, I was dying to know the scoop.

"Your aunt wanted to be the one to tell you. There's so much more at play here."

"I might bump into one and make them mad. Just tell me. I'll act surprised when Mimi brings up the subject."

She gave me a side glance. "All right, but I want to go on record that I'm telling you against my better judgment."

I couldn't help but grin. Nikki was easy to wear down and spill the tea. "Noted."

"The elemental witches can only control one aspect of nature. In comparison, the witches in our coven are multifaceted. The story goes that years ago, we all lived in harmony. A few of the elemental witch families grew jealous of the powers some of the older families possessed."

"Like the Michaels family?" A lead weight dropped to my stomach. Maybe I didn't want to know what was coming.

"Yes, and my family, too. It goes back generations. The elementals moved out of town vowing that when the coven's hierarchy weakened, they'd be back to take their rightful place and have prominent seats on the council."

"Where did they move to?"

"In and around Pine Valley."

"My parents live there."

She gave me a reassuring look. "Your mom's a Waterson."

My jaw went slack. "She's not a witch."

Nikki tipped her chin down. "No. The Waterson family's skills have diminished over the years. There are four main families, most of which have limited magic. Waterson, Erikson, Ashton, and Rockford."

"Erikson, like Gage's family?"

"Yes. They could control the air. Ashton was fire, and Rockford was earth, and of course Waterson"

"Was water." I looked out the windshield and composed my thoughts. Why wouldn't my parents have told me once I knew I was a witch?

"Don't forget your dad never told you what he was when you were growing up. They said nothing since you never exhibited signs that you were powerful in your own right."

I didn't bother to ask how she knew what I was thinking. She was always in tune with my thoughts, especially when trying to puzzle something out. "They must have assumed Mom's genes dominated." My comment was more my inner voice talking than my need to discuss it. "Why will Aunt Mimi tell me all this after the wedding?"

She gripped the steering wheel tighter. "I can't tell you that."

"Nikki."

She lifted her shoulders and dropped them. "Lily, do you trust me?"

"With my life." My heart quickened. "Is Gage in danger? Or my family?" My breath came in short gasps.

With a flick of her blinker, Nikki eased the car to the side of the road and put it in park. She took my ice-chilled hands in hers.

"Breathe in. Breathe out." She locked eyes on mine and breathed in and out very slowly.

I mimicked what she was doing.

"Good. Now, your family isn't in any danger. But there is about to be a shift in the coven's council. You must believe me when I say I am sworn to secrecy. Mimi must be the one to tell you."

"You're. Scaring. Me." I couldn't contain the quiver that laced each word.

She squeezed my hands. "I promise this is good stuff. It might be scary at first, but I'll be beside you just like since we've been kids. And when I say what's ahead is nothing compared to you solving murders, I mean it."

I nodded and forced the lump in my throat down. "Why after the wedding?"

She gazed out the window. "You've got a lot going on and don't need this on top of it."

I pressed my lips flat. "Avoiding my stare isn't going to cut it."

Her face paled. "I can't tell you. I'm sorry. I wish we never talked about the elementals. Please, don't push this any further." She wrenched her hands from mine.

I wanted to erase that pained expression from her face. "No, I'm sorry. I won't push you, and you're right. If Mimi wants to tell me, I can wait."

She threw her arms around my neck. banging her elbow on the dashboard in the process. With a wince, she said, "Thanks for understanding."

"I would never make you break a promise or, worse, go back on a vow." Satisfying my curiosity wasn't worth the anguish it was causing my best friend. "We should get back on the road. There's an ice cream bowl waiting for us."

Nikki hugged me and said, "We should go all in—skip dinner and indulge."

I laughed as she double-checked traffic before pulling back onto the highway. "Sounds good to me."

When we returned to Nikki's place, we carried the garment bags inside and hung them in her guest room closet. "Thanks for letting me keep the dresses here. I'm not about to tempt fate by having them at my house, just in case my future husband gets curious."

"You don't need to worry about Gage. That man observes every tradition and doesn't want to tempt bad luck in your direction."

"True." I tipped my head. "I think I hear Milo calling to me." I hurried to the back door, and my familiar was patiently waiting on the porch.

"We have to go back to our house. Now."

"Milo," I scooped him up. "You don't have to hang out with Murphy if you don't want to."

"It's not that. Four people have been sitting across the street from our house since before noon. We need to get back, and Mimi needs to meet us there. Nikki can drive while you call her." He trotted off the deck and paused. With a tip of his head, he said, "What are you waiting for? Time is of the essence."

"Nik," I called inside. "We need to get to my house; there are some people hanging around. Milo said I need Mimi, too. Can you drive me?"

She grabbed her bag and tossed me mine. "Did he say who it was?"

When I opened the passenger door, Milo hopped up to the console and said, "Tell Mimi it's company from Pine Valley." He placed a paw on my arm and applied pressure. "Please tell me you have your wand in your bag."

I nodded. "Yes."

"Good. Dial." He focused his attention on the windshield as Nikki drove faster than usual.

I prayed my aunt would answer the phone. On the fourth ring, I heard her say, "Cozy Nook Bookstore."

"Aunt Mimi. Milo said that you must get to my house right away. We have visitors from Pine Valley." That's when the enormity of what he said washed over me. "Four people."

She sucked in a breath. "Where are you?"

"Nikki's driving me home."

"Good. Do not engage anyone when you get there, and wait for me."

I heard a click and put my phone in my bag. "Milo, these four people are the elementals?"

He shot a sour puss face at Nikki. A similar look he'd used on me plenty of times when I didn't want to read my book, *Practical Beginnings*. "What makes you ask?"

"You asked if I have my wand. Which means they're not non-magicals waiting for me; therefore they're either witches or elementals."

"You're quick today and spot on." He stood up. "Where's the car?"

The street was empty except for regular traffic.

"Nikki, park in the driveway. We need to investigate."

Despite the heat from the mid-afternoon sun, a ripple of goosebumps raced down my arms. The breeze was heavy. The moment she parked, I was out of the car, leaving the door open. With my wand at the ready, I looked both ways on the street and hurried across, stopping my forward motion when I noticed a pool of what looked like blood.

I handed Nikki my cell phone. "Call Gage. We have a..." the sentence died on my lips.

Milo finished it. "A dead body."

Chapter 3
Gage

I smiled when I saw Lily's name on the caller ID. "Hey, Sweetheart, did you and Nikki have fun today?"

"Gage. It's Nikki. Lily's fine, but we need you to get home, to Lily's, right away. There's a dead woman across the street, and it looks like foul play was involved."

I took a deep breath. "Can I talk to Lily?"

"He wants to talk to you."

I heard the phone being fumbled with. "Gage, I'm fine."

She got that out before I could ask. "We need the group. This is definitely a murder."

"How can you tell?"

"A shard of wood is sticking out of the victim's neck, and there's a wide puddle of blood."

"The victim's dead?"

"No pulse, but the body is still warm, so it's recent."

I was already texting Peabody, Mac, and EL. The detectives and medical examiner would need to be present for this investigation.

"Send Jessie and Jonesy, too. And Gage, please hurry. A few cars have slowed as they've driven past. It's easy to guess we'll have looky-loos soon."

"We're on the way, and don't touch anything." It was my automatic response every time Lily stumbled onto a crime scene.

"I know the drill, and you know we carry gloves everywhere. And don't worry—we're safe."

"Lily, please don't get involved this time." I

was sure my pleading would fall on deaf ears, but I was going to try.

"It's too late. I have more to tell and need to talk to you in person. See you in a few minutes."

Peabody and Mac were in the lobby. "Boss," Mac said, "Peabody called EL, and he'll meet us there with the emergency team."

"Good." I pushed open the door and turned to Alice. "Any chance you can do me a favor? Call my parents and tell them I won't be stopping over after work. We've got a situation."

She gave me a thumbs up. "No problem, Detective."

I was driving down Route 1 when I finally reached the two patrol officers Lily had asked for. I figured Shepard because he was a witch, but I wasn't sure why Lily asked for Jonesy. Once they were dispatched, it was only a matter of minutes before we all converged at the crime scene.

I squeezed the steering wheel. Why did this have to happen so close to the wedding? All I wanted was an enjoyable week to ride the wave of excitement right up until Tuesday. Now Lily was hovering over a crime scene gathering clues instead of sitting on Nikki's deck relaxing in the sun.

As I made the final turn, strobing blue lights bounced off the tree-lined street. I screeched to a stop and jumped out as soon as the engine died, running to Lily as she was taking pictures on her cell phone.

Her eyes met mine. "Hi."

I slid my arm around her waist and kissed her cheek. "Hey. Want to tell me what you know?"

She focused on the female victim three feet from us. "I was at Nikki's. We'd just hung up our dresses when I heard Milo outside. He said I needed to come home right away. Four people were sitting in a car across the street. I called Aunt Mimi when Milo confirmed they were elementals."

I could feel the crease between my eyes deepen. "Who?"

"Kind of witches but with a lot less power." She looked over my shoulder. "There's Aunt Mimi now. She can explain who they are and how they are connected to us."

Nikki crossed the road to greet Mimi and spoke for several minutes. Lily didn't move to join them.

"The car was gone when you arrived?"

With a curt nod, she focused her attention on me again. "Yes. We didn't pass anyone on the way. Of course, they could have gone west, which was likely since, if they're from Pine Valley, that's the best way to go back."

Peabody strode over. "Detective, according to her driver's license, the victim is Shula Ashton from Pine Valley. There's an emergency contact listed, and when we've completed documenting the scene, Mac and I'll head to Pine Valley and inform the family."

"Thanks, Peabody." I scanned the area. "Where's Milo?"

"He's inside waiting for me." She looked at the woman's body. "Ashton, remnants of fire."

"What did you say?"

"Nothing. Her name is interesting, that's all." She clutched my hand. "Someone being killed in front of my house is not a coincidence. Especially now." Her head whipped to the right of the crime scene, and her eyes narrowed as she stared into the tree line.

"What do you mean by that, and do you see something?" Her sentence was cryptic, and blood chilled in my veins. I hated it when she said things like that. Lily was rarely wrong when her intuition twitched.

"No. I thought I saw a flash of a person, but now I'm not sure." She nodded in Mimi and Nikki's direction. "I'll let you know when I do." She kissed my cheek. "And I have all kinds of pictures. Only the area where she's lying. Once Sharon takes pictures of the entire scene, I'll need copies for my murder board."

I shook my head. "Nope. Not this time. There is no board, no sleuthing, or puzzle solving. We're getting married in a few days, and that's the only thing I want to discuss with you."

Her right eyebrow arched in dramatic fashion. "Sharon?"

Peabody came over. "Yes, Lily? How can I help?"

Crossing my arms over my chest, my feet planted wide, I said, "No. Peabody, don't answer any questions or offer to help. For once, I want to keep Lily on the sidelines of this murder investigation."

With a bland look from me to Lily, she said, "Do you think if we don't help her, Lily won't investigate? It's better to keep her in the loop so there's less chance of her finding trouble she can't handle."

I held back a small smile. With Lily's prowess in all things magic, there was very little she couldn't handle, but Peabody and Mac had no idea Lily was a witch. Now that we knew EL was a recently joined coven member, I knew he'd never share her secret. "All right, but let's make sure we keep everything going through proper channels so we have the proper chain of evidence when we catch the guilty party."

She tapped what would have been the brim of her police officer's hat but, since her promotion, she wasn't wearing one. Color flushed her cheeks as she moved away.

"Don't be so hard on her." Lily held up a hand and acknowledged EL, kneeling over the body. "I'll be back."

I thought she would go to EL, but instead, she crossed the street and strode to where Mimi and Nikki were.

"Detective, over here." Shepard waved to me and pointed to the edge of the pavement.

I reached his side and bent down. "What have you got?"

"Looks like a woman's high-heeled shoe got stuck in the soft ground. This area of the road is shaded. With the rain we had last week, it would have been easy to cause these impressions."

I squinted as I looked up. "Why do you think they're fresh?"

"Look at the leaves pushed into the holes as if the weight of a person stuck them down, and they haven't sprung back yet—not completely anyway."

I understood what he meant, and it made sense. "Excellent observation. Get plenty of pictures. Talk with EL to see if you can compare the mark to the victim's shoe." I dropped my voice. "Everything needs to be traceable in police work."

His head bobbed. "Understood, Detective."

Ah, to be eager on the job. I clapped him on the shoulder. "Keep up the good work."

He seemed to stand straighter and puffed his chest up as he beamed at the praise. "Thank you, sir."

"You don't need to call me sir." But Shepard was already absorbed in taking pictures and talking to Jonesy about making a mold of the impressions.

I stepped back and took the scene in. If

there were four people here, were they all women, and why leave a friend behind? Tires squealed down the street and screeched to a stop. Jonesy ran to intercept the three women rushing in our direction. They paused briefly to slip under the yellow crime scene tape.

I'd guess a tall woman, I'd guess six feet, strode in my direction. "Are you in charge?"

"I'm Detective Erikson. How can I help you?"

She turned to the redheaded woman. "Ravena, he's one of yours."

"Excuse me. Miss?"

"Violet Rockford." She jerked a thumb to the red-haired lady, "Ravena Erikson. The blond is Morgaine Waterson." She jabbed a finger in the direction of the victim. "That's our sister, Shula Ashton, and I want to know who did what to her and why."

I rested my hand on my holster. "Maybe you should answer a few of *my* questions first."

I held out my arm to prevent her from

storming past me. "We need to let the officers do their job to get the answers you seek."

She continued to look over her shoulder as she walked with me. "Is she dead?

"Yes." It was always best to speak the truth as simply as possible. Her lack of emotion was curious. "How is Ms. Ashton your sister?"

"We grew up together, the four of us. Our mothers used to say we were like a set of quadruplets. You know, you'd never see one without the other three." She lifted a shoulder and sighed. "I guess that's changed."

"Miss Rockford." I held up the yellow tape, and she walked under it. The other women rushed to her, wrapping arms around each other to create a tight circle of three. I could hear Violet Rockford sharing the news that their friend was dead.

Ravena Erikson started to cry and wrenched her body from the group. "I knew we shouldn't have left her here. One of us should have stayed instead of rushing off to find a restroom." The breeze kicked up as she ran down the street.

"Drama queen," Morgaine muttered and rolled her eyes. "Detective. What have you learned? Do you know who killed Shula?"

She immediately went to the top of my suspect list and glanced down her nose as if challenging me. "We've just begun our investigation, but I'm confident we will. Now, what were you doing here?"

"I don't see where that concerns you." Violet linked arms with Morgaine.

I shifted from one foot to the other under her harsh glare. I wasn't going to point out the obvious—that their friend might still be alive if they hadn't been staking out Lily's house. "I have to ask questions to get a clear picture of what happened. You can answer them here or down at the station." I paused for half a second to see if the gravity of going to the station would sink in. "Your choice."

Morgaine tightened her arm around Violet.

"We came to visit someone. But she wasn't home."

"Who?"

Ravena licked her lips, and her gaze darted to Violet. "Lily Michaels. We wanted to speak to her about a personal matter."

"Did Ms. Michaels know you were coming?"

Morgaine shook her head. "No. It was going to be a surprise."

Violet's head bobbed. "Right. Surprise." She pointed to Lily. "There she is, talking to the other women." Her hand flew to her mouth. "Could she have done it? She's powerful enough to have killed her."

Ravena rejoined them and looked around. "What's going on?"

Morgaine pointed to me. "This detective is asking us why we're here. I told him we were waiting to surprise Lily Michaels."

Violet said, "That's right. We wanted to speak with her on an important matter. It's not something we can discuss with you."

"Even if we're distant relations, we can't divulge private matters to you." Ravena linked her arm with Violet.

What was it about these three? Were they trying to draw on each other for strength? I didn't recall my family saying we had relatives in Pine Valley. That was an interesting thread to tug on. I tipped my head to the side. "Do you know anyone who might have wanted to harm Ms. Ashton?"

Violet snorted. "Stabbing is more than harming."

I leveled my gaze at her and waited.

She shifted, pulled her arm away from Ravena, and stepped forward. "I see something protruding from her neck, but I didn't put it there."

I held my ground. Intimidation wouldn't work on me. Jonesy was headed our way, accompanied by a man I'd never seen.

Violet's face dropped. "Ambrose."

"Do you know that man?"

She gulped and took a step back. "Yes. It's Shula's brother."

"Detective Erikson, this is Ambrose Ashton. He's positively identified our victim as his sister, Shula Ashton."

His eyes burned into mine. "What's happened here?"

"The investigation has just begun. I was asking these ladies a few questions."

His hands clenched into fists at his sides. "As you all appear in good health, I'm assuming you left Shula alone?"

With each clipped word he spoke, their shoulders curled over their bodies, their chins dropped lower, and their eyes glued to the ground.

Morgaine drew herself up taller but didn't look him in the eye. "We needed to use the restroom, and Shula volunteered to wait here. We were trying to talk to Lily Michaels."

"You were told that I would handle this."

She thrust her chin up. "You've been dragging your feet just like always. As council members, we took matters into our own hands."

"In the process, you got my sister killed." His laser focus was on me. "Was it a hit and run?"

I controlled my surprise that he hadn't seen the wood protruding from her neck. "It appears she died from a stab wound. I'll have specifics after the autopsy."

EL held up a hand to get my attention. I nodded. "Excuse me. I'll be right back."

When I reached his side, I asked, "What's up?"

"Preliminary report: she died from the stabbing, but the weapon is curious. It had to have been premeditated. The wood shard is extremely hard, almost petrified, and didn't come from the light wood we have around here. This was not a weapon of convenience."

"Thanks for the update. As soon as you have the report, send it over."

My four suspects were huddled together. Arms and fists were flying about, and voices were raised in anger but not loud enough so I could hear what was being said. I had to take them down to the station for individual questioning.

I scratched my head. What had been so urgent that they needed to wait outside Lily's home to talk to talk with her? I thought about their names and connection to Pine Valley. Ashton, Rockford, Erikson, and Waterson. Each name had a connection to an element of strong magic. Individually, they weren't powerful, but they might be unstoppable together— the ultimate game of rock, paper, scissors.

I looked over to Lily, talking with Mimi. Nikki was holding her hand, and Lily was shaking her head. Even from this distance, I knew something was upsetting to her.

Chapter 4
Lily

"Nope. That's not going to happen." My heart raced, and my mouth was the Mohave desert. I shook my head so hard I thought it might pop off.

Aunt Mimi took my shoulders and looked me in the eye. "Lily, this is the way it must be. The last two years have been preparing you for this exact moment."

"I can't," I wailed.

"You can and you must. You're a Michaels witch."

"Nikki?" I felt my face scrunch up, and my voice trembled. "You knew?"

She nodded. "You can do this. You're ready."

"I've been a witch for two years. In that time, I've messed up more spells than I can count. Like, remember when I was trying to turn off the light in my bedroom and instead doused the entire town?"

"A beginner's mistake, dear. We've all made them."

Aunt Mimi's calm voice didn't do anything to soothe my gurgling insides. "After you and Gage are married, there will be changes to the council. It's expected."

"But you weren't married when you assumed the role as head of the coven. Why can't you keep doing that? Down the road, when you're ready to retire, I'll feel more confident to assume my place at the table." I snapped my fingers as my eyes widened. "I can join the council and learn from you! You'll be my mentor."

She gave me an encouraging smile. "The decision has been made. The council is ready to support you, and I will still be a member—just not leading it. It will be as it should when I pass the torch to you."

My shoulders slumped. The weight of the news was almost too much to bear. "Is that why the four elementals were waiting for me? It has something to do with me becoming the head of our coven?"

Mimi's smile faltered. "I'm afraid so. Although I don't know what they hoped to gain."

Nikki snorted. "Curry favor. With the change, they might believe they'll be welcomed back to our coven."

"When I took over fifty years ago, I didn't change the bylaws. Why would they think Lily would make an exception?"

I held up a hand. "I have no idea what you're talking about. Would one of you care to fill me in?"

Nikki looked to my aunt, who asked, "How far have you read in your book?"

I threw up my hands. "Not you, too. You sound just like Milo."

Aunt Mimi said, "My dear, there's a reason why Milo has been encouraging you to read *Practical Beginnings*. There's an entire section on your role in the coven."

I stamped my foot like a child having a mini tantrum. "Why has no one ever mentioned I needed to be ready? If there had been an inkling, don't you think I would have read up on it?"

"Lily?"

I jumped at the sound of Gage's voice. "I didn't know you were behind me."

"What's wrong?"

I could see worry lines etched around his eyes. I wasn't about to add the coven news on top of his murder investigation. "Aunt Mimi told me who she thinks the people were across the street."

His brow arched. "Elemental witches from Pine Valley?"

"How did you know?"

"Lucky guess. After they told me their names and where they were from, I remembered a story my mom told me when I was a kid. It was about a group of witches who left Pembroke Cove and relocated there."

Mimi huffed. "Told to leave is more like it. Long before we were born."

"Care to fill me in tonight? I need to transport the suspects to the station for questioning."

"I'm going, too." Before he could protest, I placed a hand on his arm. "I need to know what they were doing here."

"That I can tell you. They were here to see you. They left Shula Ashton here while the other three searched for a restroom." He bobbed his head toward a tall, dark-haired man with the women. "That's her brother, Ambrose. He's angry that they took it upon themselves to come to town."

Nikki's eyebrows drew together, and Mimi bit her lower lip.

Gage asked, "What's going on?"

"I'm not sure. Why don't we ask them why

they were here to talk to me?" I strode to the middle of the road, a fair distance from where the victim had just been loaded into the ambulance. EL tapped the closed door, and the vehicle pulled away. He gave me a solemn nod, and I returned the gesture.

The women were bickering with the tall man and didn't notice my approach. I cleared my throat. "I'm Lily Michaels. I understand you wish to speak with me and were loitering outside my home." I gave each woman a stern look, reminding myself to project confidence even if I didn't feel it. I turned and addressed the man. I stuck out my hand. "You are?"

"Ambrose Ashton. Head of the council in Pine Valley."

His hand was hot as he shook mine. I pretended not to notice as I maintained contact. "Are they council members or just curiosity seekers?" I didn't care if I made him furious. They had pierced my happiness bubble of wedding fun.

"On behalf of my group, I apologize." He dipped his head but never broke eye contact.

My spine stiffened. He was not to be underestimated. "Which are they?" If I was going to be head of a witch's coven, I needed to be assertive.

What was that saying? Never let your adversary see you sweat. In this case, I was going to fake it until I made it

"Coven members, not powerful council members."

Violet said, "We are, too, council members. Ambrose fashions himself as the only member."

She stood her ground as he gave her a withering look. "We are all members, and when they learned of the upcoming leadership change, they naturally wanted to reach out to you. We hope for a more symbiotic relationship."

Did he understand what that word meant? Our coven didn't need others to survive, and membership can grow from a point of strength. Or was he trying to imply that my assuming a new role would weaken our community? This was something to mull over later. Right now, it was about that poor woman who died.

"In the process, one of your friends was killed. Can you explain who might have wanted her out of the group?" I liked it when his face paled. Had he expected me to be less formidable than my aunt? I wasn't sure where the inner strength came from, but it appeared when I needed it.

From the corner of my eye, I saw Milo perched on the edge of the road. I patted my leg, and he raced over to me, winding around my ankles until I scooped him up. His warm body steadied the jangling nerves inside of me.

Ambrose's voice cracked. "Everyone liked my sister. Her talent was extraordinary but, of course, as you know, limited."

I was missing a few details but wasn't about to betray that tidbit.

"We don't know of anyone who wished her harm. They had to have taken her by surprise, my guess, from behind to—" tears filled his eyes and he couldn't finish his sentence.

The three women circled him, murmuring words of comfort.

My heart ached for his loss, but he still hadn't said why the women wanted to speak with me specifically. "The detective needs you to go to the station to answer questions." I waved for Gage to join us. "If you still feel we need to talk, we can meet in a day or so, but I will be very busy." Investigating a murder and getting married, my plate was overfull.

The fire returned to Ambrose's eyes. "I must insist we speak today."

"I'm sorry you feel that way. At the moment, my focus is the untimely death of a young woman. Not my new role." I narrowed my eyes. "I'm surprised finding who's responsible isn't your first concern."

"Of course I want to know what happened to my sister. I have many people counting on me to solicit your help."

"We'll talk. Just not today." I nodded to Gage. "I'll see you later."

I carried Milo to the house and nodded to Nikki and my aunt to follow me.

He grumbled. "My dear witch, well done."

Before I went to the station, I had to set up my murder board. If this murder was somehow related to my ascension as coven leader, I needed to solve it before I reluctantly took my place at the center of that formidable table.

Milo was perched on the kitchen table, Aunt Mimi and Nikki each took a chair, and I stood in front of my clue board. I had written Shula Ashton's name in the middle, with a circle around it. Like spokes on a bicycle tire, I listed Violet, Ravena, Morgaine, and Ambrose's names.

"Each person represents one element in magic, if we dissect their names as an indicator." I consulted my laptop. "Who would have motive to kill Shula? You know the killer has to be someone from Pine Valley—specifically, one of them. Off the top of my head, the three women can alibi each other, so Gage will need to push hard on that during questioning." I paused and jotted a text to let him know I'd be there shortly and to stall.

"How did Ambrose know to come here? Pine Valley is at least a thirty-minute drive."

Nikki said, "He either knew the ladies were here, or he killed his sister." She shuddered and dropped her voice. "Is that even possible?"

Aunt Mimi placed her hand on Nikki's. "I think he's the least likely to have done the deed. Family protects family. And by the murderous look he gave the three women when he saw his sister laying on the ground, he suspects one of them."

"Before we head down the rabbit hole of who could have done this, why did they need to see me? Details, please." I gave Aunt Mimi my best imitation of Gage waiting for a suspect to crack.

When she didn't say a word and kept her eyes glued to the floor, Milo cleared his throat.

"My dear witch. As the new head of the Pembroke Cove witches' coven, neither Mimi nor Nikki wants to say that you have the power to listen as the elementals plead their case to be readmitted to our coven."

"Just listening? That doesn't seem like a big deal. A conversation between witches." I looked at Nikki. "Am I missing something?"

She leaned forward, her arms resting on the table. "If they were to be allowed back in, they could combine their powers to overthrow the peace our coven has had for decades."

Aunt Mimi slapped her hand on the table.

I jumped. "Whoa. Aunt Mimi, are you against letting them address the council?"

"We haven't heard from them in almost fifty years. They didn't try to come before the council when I was the coven head, so why now? They could be up to no good."

"We're jumping to conclusions that can't be substantiated at this time. We know they want to talk with me, and I'll listen. If I take over the coven, I'll not turn my back on anyone—witch or non-magical alike."

Nikki nodded. "You're right. But first, we need to kick up our heels at your wedding and then get you inducted as head of the coven. After that, you can deal with the Pine Valley contingent."

I shook my head. "No. The first thing we do is solve who killed Shula Ashton and why. Which might dovetail into why these witches have decided now is the time to talk to me." My face scrunched. "How did they know about me at all?"

"It's written in the charter that the next Michaels witch would take over from me. If you had never come into your powers, your child would have. Magic never skips two generations."

"I'm marrying a non-magical. Our child could inherit from Gage's mother."

Mimi shook her head. "She comes from a

long line of powerful witches. It was just a matter of time." Tears filled her eyes, and I hoped they were happy ones. "I'm so glad it's you. Your compassion and living as a non-magical for years gave you balance. Which is critical in your new role."

"In other news," Milo grumbled, "as your familiar, I will be recognized as an asset. At one time, I had been head of the coven before my unfortunate circumstance." He held up a paw. "Which we'll not rehash."

"And what about Gage? How will he fit into all of this?"

Mimi quirked a brow. "I'm not sure what you're asking. He won't suddenly inherit magic. Glinda's sure he's non-magical, but after the wedding, he'll have the ability to communicate with Milo."

I perked up. "Like, understand when Milo is talking to him?"

Milo groaned. "I forgot that tidbit. But yes, Detective Cutie will be able to understand me, but only when I speak directly to him. He won't hear everything I say, so I can still poke fun at him and call him DC."

I tapped my finger to my lips. "There might be pluses to this new role that could be viewed as perks."

"Exactly." Nikki grinned. "That's the way to look at it."

My cell pinged with an incoming message from Gage. I scanned it. "Gage says I need to get to the station if I want to observe him questioning the suspects. He can't stall any longer."

I tapped OK and hit the send button. "This conversation is tabled for the moment. Now that I know about the coven, we won't talk to anyone until I fill Gage in."

Aunt Mimi said, "I should be with you when you do. He'll have questions you won't be able to answer."

I pursed my lips and nodded. "Agreed." I waved the board back into the pantry closet and said, "I'm going to put a protective bubble around the crime scene while we're gone. Even with the police processing the scene, I want it to be preserved until Nikki and I can take another look."

She let out a huge exhale. "Does this mean you're not upset with me for knowing and not telling you what's coming?"

I crossed the room and hugged her. "I'm not mad but promise me that when this is all over, there will be no more coven secrets between us."

She held her right hand up. "I promise."

"Then, as my brilliant friend, we need to get to the station and see what we can learn to solve this murder in record time."

She nodded. "Maybe then we can have those sundaes we talked about."

It seemed like weeks since we imagined spooning decadent bowls of ice cream while relaxing on her deck. "That's my plan."

Aunt Mimi stood. "I'm going to make a few inquiries to see what I can learn about the visitors and what they hoped to accomplish by staking out your home. When I know something, I'll text you."

I kissed her cheek. "Thank you, Aunt Mimi. I know I can always count on you."

Chapter 5
Lily

I parked the Mini Coop at the station and looked at Nikki. "Is there anything else I should know before we go inside?"

"No. You had Mimi take care of the preservation spell over the crime scene and let Jessie Shepard know what she was doing. For the record, you could have done it with solid intention."

"I meant about everything else."

She wrapped her pinky around mine like she did when we were kids. "I swear. You taking over for Mimi is the only thing I've ever held back from you, well, and I was sure you were a witch even when you didn't know. But you must come into magic on your own. It can't be forced, or it goes wonky. Once you had Milo in your corner, it was only a matter of time."

"You knew Milo was my familiar?"

She nodded. "He and Murphy bonded right away."

"Two familiars ratting me out." I shook my head. "What other interesting facts will I learn today?" I opened the car door and got out. The parking lot at the station was empty except for Sharon and Mac's police-issued sedan, parked next to Gage's.

I looked at Nikki over the roof of my car. "Ready?"

"Ready, Sherlock." With two simple words, Nikki reminded me of my talent for solving puzzles.

"Let's go." I grinned. All this talk of me assuming a role in the coven, let alone *the role*, evaporated. My fingertips tingled at the thought of discovering clues for this latest murder. I was sobered by the realization a woman lost her life today, but justice would be done. We'd uncover who had committed this horrible crime, and Gage would make sure they paid the consequences.

The back door to the station opened, and Shepard stood on the step. "There you are. Detective Erikson sent me to find you."

I hurried over with Nikki on my heels. "Sorry, I put together my clue board and Mimi added a spell to the crime scene." I gave him a puzzled look. "Weren't you just there?"

He leaned forward. "Don't say anything, but I did a time bending spell so I could talk to you."

"Oh?"

"The woman who was killed was a fire witch. The three others are also versed in magic; air, earth, and water."

I didn't have the heart to tell him I knew this information. As far as Jessie knew, this was an unfortunate situation. His loyalty to share the facts with me was touching.

"That's good to know. Is there anything else that was discovered?"

He frowned. "Not yet. EL is working on the case, and he's the best at processing evidence. I'll let you know when something comes up from the scene."

"Jessie, don't put yourself on the line for me. I've been pretty good at sussing out clues."

His face went bright pink. "I'm sorry, I was trying to help."

I placed my hand over my heart. "I appreciate that. It would be best if you didn't get in trouble because of me. Gage doesn't tell me most of the information, either. I usually find out, and then he confirms it."

He nodded. "That makes sense. You're good at solving riddles. Like when I heard about the magician that left you clues in book titles. That was way cool." He held the door, and we walked inside.

I wasn't about to admit that those particular clues almost got past me since several didn't fit a logical pattern. We walked down the stuffy hall; the heat and humidity clung to my skin. As we approached the conference rooms, the air cooled. Jessie held open the door to the observation room. We stepped inside and pulled chairs in front of the one-way mirror. Gage was sitting with Violet Rockford.

She took a tissue from the box he held out and blew her nose. "I'm sorry, Detective, this situation caught me off guard. Shula was a good friend, more like a sister."

"I understand this must be very difficult. In my experience, people often notice little things that at the time don't make any sense but can be important clues."

He glanced in the direction of the mirror and gave an imperceptible nod. Almost as if he sensed I was there. I placed my hand on the mirror, and it warmed under my hand. I wasn't sure what motivated me to do that, but he smiled.

"Jessie, Gage couldn't see my hand, could he?"

"No. I clicked on the camera, so I'm sure he figured out you're in here now."

"Technology is a good tool in this type of case." I sank into the chair and waited for Gage to ask his first question.

"Violet. Why did you and the others decide to wait for Lily? What was so urgent that you had to speak with her today?"

"We wanted to congratulate her on your upcoming wedding." Her eyes widened. "You are the groom, right?"

"Have you met before?"

She shook her head. "No, but we have people in common. A wedding is a very special time in a girl," she stuttered, "a woman's life. We wanted her to know she's an inspiration to all single ladies."

"Ha." I glanced at Nikki. "She can't tell him the truth because he's a non-magical, and she believes he has no idea I'm a witch."

"Would you marry someone if they didn't know the truth?"

"Not me, and in your case, Steve knew for years before you tied the knot."

Jessie said, "I'm not going to date any girl seriously for a long time, so I don't need to worry about that."

I grinned. "Take your time and find the right one. Look at Gage and me: it took us years."

Nikki poked my leg. "Gage is giving Violet that long stare."

I turned my attention back to the interview in progress.

"I'm sure Lily appreciates the gesture. How long had you been waiting?"

She looked at the ceiling tiles and twirled a curl around her finger. "We got there before lunch. Ravena had us stop at Robin's Café in town, and we ordered sandwiches to go."

I made a note to check in with Regan to see when the women picked up their meal. A group of women always stood out to her; she had a memory like an elephant.

"I wanted to go to the Copper place, but the line was so long, and I needed to use the restroom." Violet shrugged. "The sandwiches were good, and we had lemonade. Why on earth we got the large size is beyond me. What goes in? Well, you catch my drift." She gave him a pointed look.

Gage nodded. "Did you see anyone drive by more than once while you were waiting for Ms. Michaels?"

"No. That street's deadsville. Why Lily Michaels would want to live there is a mystery to me."

"What time did you leave Shula to go into town?"

"Oh, we didn't come back into town. Morgaine wanted to swing by the beach. The ocean is her place, and they have public restrooms in the parking area. So, we went there. Everyone was happy, and Morgaine got to walk in the waves. It's the little things that bring joy, you know."

"Did anyone see you while you were there?"

"It was crowded, but it wasn't like we chatted anyone up to give us an alibi. Is that what you're getting at?"

"It would be helpful if we can verify your claim."

"Don't you have cameras around that building? We'd show up on that."

I shifted in my chair. "Clever girl."

Nikki said, "She's got a quick answer for everything."

"She does, and mentioning the camera is a good point." I looked over my shoulder. "Jessie, is that something you can mention to Sharon or Mac? It'd be good to see the footage."

"I'll take care of that right now. Then, I'm going to head back out to the crime scene. I've been gone long enough."

"Thanks again for everything, Jessie."

He smiled as he left.

Nikki waited until the door closed before saying, "Someone has a case of hero worship."

My cheeks grew warm. "No, he doesn't. He's just a nice person and a good cop."

"Right." She drawled the word out and grinned. "And I'm a terrible baker."

Gage tapped a pen on his pad. I pointed to what was happening on the other side of the mirror.

"What time do you think you left Shula?"

She narrowed her eyes. "I don't like the way you said we left her. Shula volunteered to stay so we wouldn't miss our chance with Lily. We were gone maybe thirty minutes more or less."

"What time did you leave?"

"I didn't look at the clock. I'd guess a half hour before we got back." She folded her arms across her body and lowered her chin. The ground rippled under us. "I did not hurt Shula. She was like family."

"You can't think of anyone that would want to hurt her?"

She shook her head, causing her curls to swing like ropes. "Not a single person."

He jotted a note and casually looked up. "Please give your contact information to the other detectives on your way out."

She shoved the chair back and rose to her feet. "You're wasting time talking to us. I'll bet Ambrose knows more than we do." She stomped from the room and Gage looked in my direction.

I pushed the speaker button on the wall. "Jessie will let Sharon and Mac know about the beach."

"Good. I expect the next two interviews to be similar. Then I'll chat with Ambrose last."

I pressed the button again. "We're staying."

Gage turned to the door, and Ravena Erikson strolled in with a smirk. She held out her hand. "Cousin."

"Detective will be just fine."

She lifted her shoulder and sat down. "Detective, why do you deny our connection?"

"Lots of people share last names but have zero connection to each other. Take, for example, Smith." He lifted a brow and gave her a long look. "Would you suggest every person around the globe named Smith is related?"

"Of course not. But these circumstances are," she wrinkled her nose, "different."

"We should talk about today."

"As you wish, cousin."

He didn't react to the word, but I was sure he was curious whether they were related—a question for his parents at another time. He asked her the same questions he'd asked Violet, but in a different order.

"Is Gage trying to see if their stories match?"

"Yes. Have you noticed her responses are identical to Violet's? Almost rehearsed."

She nodded. "Good observation."

I leaned closer.

"Did you go into the ocean, too?"

"No. I'm not drawn to it like Morgaine. Instead, I savored the ocean breeze. You know that saltiness and the undercurrent of cool air was a balm to my weary soul."

He made a note and didn't look up when he asked, "What time did you leave Shula and come back into town?"

"Around two."

I slapped my hand against my leg. "We found the body at three. Therefore, it was longer than a half hour if Ravena is to be believed. Also, that means the time of death was between two and two forty-five since Milo needed time to get to your place."

Gage said, "Did you see anyone in the area while you were parked?"

"The usual pickup trucks, delivery vans, you know, normal happenings. But there was a dark SUV that drove by twice. I thought it was odd. It had black-out windows like you'd see down south."

"And you didn't recognize the vehicle."

"Nope. Are we done?"

"Yes, thank you. Confirm your contact details with an officer."

"You got it, cuz. Do yourself a favor and look up your family tree. You'll see we're related from way back when."

She sailed from the room without a backward glance.

The moment she was gone, Morgaine Waterson drifted in. "Detective. Violet's already told you exactly what happened. We got lunch, drank too much of a sugary beverage, and went to the ocean, where I was able to refresh my spirit with a quick walk through the surf."

He cocked a brow. "What time did you go to the ocean?"

She tapped a short, manicured fingernail polished in a light blue on her lips. "Somewhere after lunch and when we got back. I'm just terrible with time. I go by my internal clock. Just ask anyone. Before you ask, I didn't see anyone hanging around that woman's house, either. Except for a gray kitty, which was so cute but refused to cross the street so I could pet it."

"Nikki, why would she want to pet Milo? She knows I'm a witch. It's not a stretch to assume he's my familiar."

"My guess is to sway his opinion of them."

Once again, Gage asked Morgaine to provide her contact information to the officers out front. She stood and Ambrose strode in.

"If you're done questioning these women, I'd like to tell you what I know so we can go home. I must tell the family what's happened before they find out via the wild vine network."

Nikki said, "He means the grapevine."

He dragged the chair out and sat down, one leg propped over the other knee. He flexed his fingers, drawing them into fists.

I stood and took a step toward the one-way mirror.

His head spun in my direction and his eyes burned into mine. Did he feel me watching him?

Nikki grabbed my arm and pulled me back. "He's on the edge of losing control."

I nodded, my lips forming a thin line. Placing my hand against the mirror, I concentrated on Gage. *From the depths of my soul, I wrap Gage in my protection as if I stand between him and harm. For this I wish, so it shall be.*

Ambrose grinned and then inclined his head in my direction. He turned to Gage. "You want to know what I know?"

He placed his hands palm down on the table. "Yes. Let's start at the beginning. Why did you come to Pembroke Cove?"

He thrust his cell phone across the table. "I got this text from Shula. As you can see, she was concerned after they abandoned her on the side of the road."

Gage scanned the phone and wrote down what I assumed was the message. He gave the phone to Ambrose. "The timestamp is two o'clock."

"I didn't get it until forty-five minutes later. I was in a meeting." With a sharp thrust of his chin, he eyed Gage. "One of those witches killed my sister and, for their sake, you'd better find out which one before I do."

Chapter 6
Gage

My pulse picked up. I had seen Ashton's type before. He'd go off half-cocked and innocent people usually ended up caught in the crossfire. "Mr. Ashton, don't take the law into your own hands. I promise you that the person responsible will be held accountable. My team is excellent at what they do."

He leaned forward, his hands curled into fists on the table. "If the Pembroke Cove police department is so great, how could a young woman have been killed in your town?"

I wanted to point out that police officers couldn't read minds. But I closed my eyes momentarily and put myself in his shoes. He was lashing out after just learning his sister had been murdered. "I am profoundly sorry this happened. To reassure you, I'll do all I can to put the guilty person behind bars."

His shoulders slumped, and he hung his head. "Shula was my little sister, always following me like my shadow. I used to tell her to knock it off, but secretly, I liked that she looked up to me." He lifted his head, his eyes water-filled. "Those women used to argue all the time, and over everything. Dates, clothes, magic, you name it, they fought about it. It was Morgaine's idea to seek out Lily Michaels. Shula told them to wait until after the ceremony, but when Morgaine made a decision, Violet and Ravena would take her side and expect Shula to fall in line."

"Doesn't sound like they respected her opinion."

His voice was flat. "Ya think? I tried to tell

her to stand up for herself but she didn't see them for what they really were."

I waited. Ambrose was on a roll, and I wasn't about to slow down his stream of consciousness.

"Shula wanted to believe the best in every person she met. No one ever had an ulterior motive. She held up a mirror and everyone was as kind as she was. It was maddening. Most people were a reflection of her, at least when they encountered her. For someone to stab her in the back, isn't that the greatest betrayal? Doesn't it mean it had to have been someone she knew?"

"It's a possibility."

"That's why it has to be one of those twits." A shudder raced over him. He took shallow yet audible breaths, let out a loud sigh, and pinched his eyes shut, pressing his fingers to them. The shock was wearing off, and now the grief would wash over him in a new wave of emotion.

"Can I call someone for you?"

He hung his head. "No. If I can have a moment, I'll answer the rest of your questions."

"Coffee, water?"

"No. Thank you."

The minutes ticked off on the wall clock and I would give him the time he needed. The grief was genuine, or he was an Oscar-worthy actor.

After several minutes, he lifted his head; his eyes were vacant, and his voice was flat. "What else do you need to know."

"Would your sister have volunteered to stay behind when the others left to use a restroom?"

He shook his head. "No. They're stronger together." He held up his phone again. "Something or someone caused her to be concerned."

The stronger together comment was curious, but I kept pressing forward. "Do you think Morgaine would have wanted to dip her toes in the ocean?"

"Yes."

"Why do you think Shula didn't tell you what was upsetting her?"

His eyes were cold. "How should I know? Maybe she thought I'd drive too fast to get to her? I wish I had the answer. I'm going to spend the rest of my life wondering."

"Other than the three women she was with, is there anyone else you can think of who would want to harm her?"

"No. Like I said, she was a sweetheart. Is there anything else? I must get home."

I pushed back my chair and stood, extending my hand. "I'm very sorry for your loss."

He hesitated before shaking mine with a burning, vise-like grip. "Just find out who's responsible, and I'll make sure we honor Lily's decision. Whatever it is."

He left the room and I looked at the one-way mirror. "Lily, can you come in here, please?" I sat and thought about my suspects, Ambrose's cryptic final words, and what these women were doing waiting outside Lily's home.

Lily and Nikki entered the conference room and Nikki closed the door. Lily sat down and pulled out a chair for Nikki next to her.

The vein in Lily's neck pulsed. This was not going to be good news.

"Can you tell me what the heck is going on with these people from Pine Valley and their connection to you?"

"I'm not entirely sure what they hoped to accomplish by talking to me, but I have news."

The way she phrased the statement, it was almost as if she expected me to interrogate her like a suspect. "Sweetheart, just tell me what's going on. I won't be able to solve this case unless I have all the facts."

Her head bobbed. "Aunt Mimi wants to be with me when I tell you."

I glanced at Nikki. "Can you shed light on this secondary mystery?"

She shook her head. "I'm sworn to secrecy since you're a non-magical."

Well, at least that answered one thing. This was about witches and the coven. A couple of months ago, Jessie mentioned that Lily would take over the coven. I dismissed the idea then, but maybe I should have asked more questions.

"Text Mimi and ask her to come down, and then we'll discuss what you can share regarding the women and Ambrose."

Lily tapped the screen on her phone, and I heard the soft *whoosh* as she hit send. "We heard Ambrose talking in cryptic sentences from time to time. It wasn't because he was grief-stricken. He and the other three are elemental witches from Pine Valley."

I frowned. "That I gathered. The one, Ravena, even thinks we're related."

"Well," Nikki began, "you might be. Erikson isn't a common name in this part of the country. Until today, had you met anyone around here with the same last name?"

I hadn't thought of that, and she was right, but there was no way I could be a long-lost cousin of that woman. She was odd. "I guess it's possible."

Lily pointed to Nikki. "We've been thinking. Based on their names, they must represent the four elements—water, fire, earth, and air."

Leaning back in my chair, I ran a hand over

my head. "Makes sense. Nik, did you know elemental witches lived in the next town?"

"Yes. But I'm not friends with anyone in Pine Valley besides Lily's parents." She glanced at Lily. "We, the witches of Pembroke Cove, and the elementals keep our distance. There was a feud decades ago. I don't know if anyone cares anymore. But from what I've seen today, they're rude and obnoxious."

Lily tapped the tabletop. "Until today, I might have had a customer come into the store from there, but we never crossed paths socially."

"Then why were four women waiting to talk to you? What was so urgent that they were loitering outside of your home?"

The door burst open and Mimi closed it behind her. "Don't answer that." She held her palms up to the ceiling. "I wish to block all sound and keep our conversation room bound. No one else needs to fear the secrets that we're about to hear. Create a bubble around us now until I bring it down. For this I wish, so it shall be." She wiped her hands on her slacks. "It's not perfect, but it will do under these circumstances."

She kissed my cheek. "Hello, dear." She sat next to me. I was always surprised by how much Lily and her aunt looked alike. They had the same petite frame, sable brown eyes, and a smattering of freckles; but Mimi's hair, which had once been chestnut brown, had grown to a soft gray.

I looked at the three women around the table. "Will someone tell me what's going on? It's like I'm watching a foreign language movie with no subtitles."

Mimi patted Lily's hand. "Let me take these questions."

She nodded. "Okay."

"Many years ago, long before I took over the coven, we had members from Pine Valley who were elemental witches. They differ from us as they each can control one power. Together, they're extremely powerful if they harness their magic correctly. But they didn't like to follow the rules of the coven, especially our primary directive, which is, *do no harm*. Some of the elemental witches used their powers to create mischief. Pranks that were borderline mean."

Lily leaned forward. I guessed this was new information for her, too.

"Of course, disciplinary action was taken." She sighed. "It only made matters worse. The council met and decided to ban them from our meetings. Some were concerned that the growing hostility between full witches and the elementals could lead to uncontrolled bad magic, which wouldn't be good for the non-magicals in our towns. We take our responsibility as members of the community very seriously. It was then we fractured into two groups; full-blood witches stayed in Pembroke Cove and elementals relocated to Pine Valley."

"Was it hostile?"

"No. Not exactly. In the early years, we had to do some corrective spells in the county. Eventually, life smoothed out and we've coexisted for years without any issue."

I didn't bother to take notes since this couldn't be entered as evidence for the case. "Why are they here now, waiting to talk to Lily?"

She turned in her chair to face me. "This has caught us off guard. We would have made arrangements if we had anticipated any of them seeking out Lily."

My gut twisted. "Mimi. Using your words, what kind of arrangements?"

"Well, we would have talked to her about what would happen after your wedding. The entire council agreed to wait until then."

"The council, like my mom, was aware of these conversations?"

"Dear, she's a council member, but remember, like all witches, Glinda's sworn to secrecy."

I slammed my hand on the table. "When it comes to my future wife, there is no room for secrets. She has a knack for finding danger. How often do we need to come close to losing her before the council thinks about her safety before their secrets? What if these women had been lying in wait to harm her?"

"They wouldn't have done that. They wanted to talk to her and get her on their side before your wedding." Mimi's soothing voice didn't quell the panic rising in my chest.

I rubbed my sternum. "Mimi. I don't like where this conversation is going."

Nikki said, "Just wait. You won't like the next bit of news any better."

I placed my palms on the table and stood, my feet planted wide. I looked at Mimi, Nikki, and then Lily. "I don't appreciate being kept out of the information loop."

Lily said, "I learned about this before coming to the station. I've been in the dark, too."

Mimi touched my hand. "Gage, please sit down. This will be a lot to absorb, and we wanted to tell you both in a way that made sense; but in light of today's events, we can't wait for the perfect time."

"Who's we?" I returned to my seat. Mimi asked.

"The council, including Glinda, Burke, Reed, and Mindy. We thought it best for you to have the support of your parents as the next steps unfold."

At least they included our parents. "Mimi, you've dragged this out long enough. Tell me. Now."

She nodded to Lily. "After your marriage, I will retire as head of the coven and Lily will take my place."

My wife, head of the coven? I turned to Lily, my mouth dry, my voice strained as I asked, "And you had no idea?"

She shook her head. "No. I'm still having trouble wrapping my head around it."

I clenched my hands together and stared at the table. "What does that mean exactly?" My heart thudded. I knew the head of the coven had to be a very powerful witch. Which also meant that she could be vulnerable to every underhanded witch far and wide.

"Gage, sweetheart. It won't change a thing. I'll still have my bookstore, and we'll have our own life. I need to run meetings every month." Her gaze darted to Mimi. "Right, Aunt Mimi?"

She tipped her head from one side to the other. "More or less."

Nikki stood and perched on the table, her feet on the chair she had just vacated. "Look. Mimi isn't going to come clean on the nitty-gritty details, so I will."

Mimi sniffed and folded her hands in her lap. "If you think this is a good time to fill Lily and Gage in on a few niggle details, go for it."

"They have the right to know." Nikki focused her attention on me and Lily. "What this means is Lily has become a mighty witch, stronger than Mimi or anyone else in the coven."

"But I'm not." Lily glanced at me; her brows were drawn together and her face was ghostly white.

"You are. As your best friend, I will be your right hand in the coven. I can feel your power when you do magic: it's like the sun on a perfect summer day. It doesn't feel hot and uncomfortable. An extra surge of energy filters into the community; nothing bad happens, it's thrilling. Milo's done an amazing job preparing you in a few short years to take on this role. Once you and Gage marry, Glinda's magic will blend with yours to enhance it even more."

This was beyond my comprehension. "I'm not a witch."

"No. But you live the directive every day. *Do no harm.* More importantly, you love Lily. Haven't you wondered why Lily finally opened her book, *Practical Beginnings*, at that precise moment?"

She asked, "When I fell and hit my head?"

Nikki didn't respond; she took Lily's hand. "Tell me, around that time, didn't you start to think about a deeper relationship with her, that you loved her?"

"How did you? Are you saying it was our change in relationship that catapulted her discovery of magic?"

"That, and adopting Milo."

"Wait just a minute." Lily grabbed my hand. "Our relationship has nothing to do with my becoming a witch."

"Love is the most powerful magic, my dear niece. It's time you take your place as head of the council. I have the utmost confidence that you'll do great things. The coven will flourish under your guidance."

I kissed Lily's hand.

She pulled away and paced from one side of the room to the other.

Silence blanketed us. I needed time to process the fact that Lily would be head of the coven. What little I knew meant monthly meetings, an occasional business meeting, and the head of the council made sure that magic was used appropriately. Could that be dangerous? "How many witches know Lily will assume her place after our wedding?"

Mimi's voice was strong and steady. Like in a *don't question this* attitude. "Anyone who's read the charter knows the succeeding head of the coven will be a Michaels witch and will assume control when their powers exceed the current head of the coven."

Lily gasped. "To be clear, you've always known I would be a witch, and I'm now connected to Glinda's magic by marrying Gage? Who the heck am I going to call when I mess up a spell?"

Chapter 7
Lily

I broke out in a cold sweat. "Aunt Mimi, there is no way my powers exceed yours. Look at how you saved Milo. I couldn't have done that. There's just..."

Aunt Mimi's smile was gentle. "My dear girl, you're more than ready. You can't see it because you aren't looking at your powers objectively. The council has been watching your progress. There has never been another witch who's learned to fly as quickly as you."

"That was all Barry Shepard's skill at teaching." I sat on my trembling hands to prevent anyone from realizing I had gone from scared to terrified. "And I hardly ever read my book, *Practical Beginnings*. Milo's always nagging me —*read the book, Lily*. And remember, if I were up on reading it, I would have known about the fairies and nymphs and the elemental witches and that I was going to take control after the wedding. But nope, I ignore the lessons."

Nikki said, "Take a breath, Lily. It wasn't time for you to know about the other beings in Pine Valley." As a gentle reminder, she said, "You've been busy with the wedding and running the bookstore."

Gage said, "Not to mention the murders you've solved, even one just a few weeks ago." He was nodding, but his face was a new shade of pale, one I'd never seen before.

"Lily, you're constantly creating spells on the fly that work. Your intention and focus are admirable. Most witches can never accomplish that quick thinking and are literal regarding their spells. That's talent and power."

"If I'd been reading the book, would I have

known the elemental witches would come to town?"

"The book doesn't tell you the future, just teaches you what you need to know."

Despite Aunt Mimi's reassurance, my gut clenched. I sagged against the back of the chair, and my knees knocked. I'd be slumped on the floor if I weren't sitting down.

"This is overwhelming."

Aunt Mimi nodded, her empathy washing over me. "I'm sure, but unfortunately, a woman lost her life today, and before you and Gage get married, it needs to be resolved. You can't have something like this hanging over you."

"Why did they really come to see me?" My gaze slid from Nikki to my aunt. "Do you know?"

"This was something I'd hoped we could talk about at the first meeting, but that option has been taken from us." Aunt Mimi took my hands in hers. "They're hoping you reinstate their membership into the coven. With your lack of exposure to the past, they're counting on it working in their favor."

"How can I do that? I'd have to understand the issues that led to them leaving and what has changed in the years since, other than a new generation of elemental witches coming to the meetings."

Nikki smiled at my aunt. "This is my best friend, the fair and level-headed Lily. Never one to make a snap judgment or decision, and that's why she'll be great for the council."

"Aunt Mimi, I'd like you to call a council meeting tonight, if possible. If I'm going to be charged with making important decisions, I need access to what has transpired. Only then will I talk with anyone from Pine Valley who wishes to see me."

"I'll see what I can do."

Nikki grinned. "Spoken like a born leader."

My heart thumped in an unnatural rhythm as my voice squeaked. "Doesn't the council make decisions as a group, like majority rules?"

"Of course, but in the case of a tie, the head

witch is the tiebreaker. You're the only one who can direct the council to investigate issues. And in the event of an emergency, your magic will protect the coven, should that become necessary."

I swallowed hard and a bead of sweat ran down my spine. This sounded more intense with each passing sentence. I waved my hand and stared at the floor. "Enough talk of power and magic."

Gage said, "Ladies, may I have a few minutes with Lily?"

Nikki and my aunt's chairs scraped across the floor as they stood. I heard the door open and close. Gage's arms wrapped around my hunched body. He didn't speak but held me close.

My body relaxed and I slipped my arms around his neck. "I'm so sorry."

He eased my chin up and looked me in the eyes. "For what? Being extraordinary?"

I shook my head. "I'm not."

"My favorite and beautiful witch, you are

that and much more, if possible. We'll be married in a few days, and knowing you'll be head of the coven makes me burst with pride."

My eyebrows slid together. "It does?"

"Of course. I love you with all my heart. Knowing that you'll guide the next generations of witches with compassion, logic, and fairness makes me wish I could shout it from the rooftops."

"I never thought about helping others." The clenching of my tummy was receding, and my heart rate returned to normal. I straightened in my chair. "I like the idea of helping other witches, but first, we must figure out what happened to Shula Ashworth. When we do, it could go a long way to soothe the strained relationship between the witches of Pine Valley and Pembroke Cove."

"Don't you mean the elementals and witches?"

I tipped my head and gave him a look he knew meant I had a different idea. "Elemental witches and full powered witches shouldn't be treated differently. We all have something to contribute. That's the first misconception that will be cleared up if it's an issue to anyone in either community." I pecked his lips. "As a non-magical who is part of our community, I know you understand."

A broad grin graced his lips, and his hazel eyes sparkled. "I like it when you get all fired up."

"Good, then let's get fired up about poor Shula."

He cupped my cheek. "Before we do, can I remind you I can't wait for us to be married?"

"Good. Now, get the gang together and meet at my house. There's a clue board waiting to be filled in, and the lucky part is that the crime scene is right across the street. I think before dinner, we should take another look."

He shook his head. "Only you can make discussing murder sound like an adventure."

The smile slipped from my face. "I take the loss of life very seriously. Having our friends gather to discuss it over a meal does two things

—it keeps the conversation and theories flowing, and being part of the group means no one bears the burden alone."

Nikki drove me home. It was a quiet ride, as I was lost in thoughts of assuming a spot, no *the* spot, on the council. How could I, a bookstore owner and novice witch, be the head of anything, let alone the most important council in this part of Maine?

"You know, you're not in this alone."

I looked at Nikki. "But I am."

"Holmes never has to be without Watson."

"This is different, Nikki. I have no idea what to expect." I twisted my shoulder bag strap in my hands. "That doesn't matter right now. We have a murder to solve, and the rest of this council business will come later."

"Right. So, what do you want to do first?"

"Take another look at the crime scene and

set up the clue board. Gage will take care of dinner and invite everyone over."

She nodded. "I've texted Steve. He'll be at the house when we get back."

"Good." I looked at the scenery out the window. "Aunt Mimi cast the protection spell over the spot, so we can get a good look."

"Do you think Gage will keep the police onsite overnight?"

"No. Once they've finished processing it, I'm sure he'll release the scene. Unless there's compelling evidence he thinks needs to be protected." I wrinkled my brow. "Do you remember seeing a handbag anywhere on the side of the road?"

"No, but she might not have carried one, especially since she wasn't driving. Sometimes, when you drive, I bring my cell phone and debit card."

"House keys?"

She laughed softly. "I lock my house with magic like you do. Shula might not have that skill, so I'd guess she'd have keys on her."

"Which makes more sense that she'd have some kind of bag, even if it's small, for money, keys, and a phone."

"True. We can ask Jessie if they found one."

I closed my eyes and pictured the site again. "Unless it was found in the wood part behind the body, she didn't have one. That's a question we need answered."

Nikki pulled into the driveway and we got out. "I want to check on Brutus and see if Milo noticed anything while we were gone."

"I'll come in, too. I don't want to go across the street without you."

Once inside, I called out, "Milo. Brutus?" The door to the pantry was ajar.

"About time you got home." Milo slunk out of the pantry closet. "I'm hungry, and you might want to sweep up the bag of dog treats I accidentally knocked on the floor." He sat and glared at me. "Why does that big lug of a dog have cookies and I don't?"

"Milo. You're exhausting at times." With a flick of my wrist, the dustpan and broom made quick work of the spilled treats. "You gave up store-bought treats months ago. You said you deserved real food like smoked salmon, not the pressed treats that looked like cartoon fish."

"True. But there's no smoked salmon in there, either."

I pulled open the refrigerator door. "That's because I store it here, or I'd never have any in the house."

He swished his tail from side to side. "Can I have some now? Then I promise to tell you what I saw while you were gone."

I picked Milo up and set him on the chair. "Information first, and then we'll have snacks."

"Fine." He gazed longingly at the refrigerator door. "After Mimi took care of the protection spell, those two cops, Jonesy and Shepard, circled the yellow tape every few minutes, guarding the scene. Occasionally, a car would drive by and slow down, typical of a gawker, but they'd wave them by. Then, those three witches who went to the station for questioning returned. Two chatted up

Jonesy, but the third talked with Shepard for quite some time. He kept shaking his head and pointing to the car they came in. Finally, one woman threw up her hands and stomped back to the car, and the other two followed her. After they left, the victim's brother stopped. He talked with the two cops and another heated argument took place, which, for the record, that dude has one short temper," Milo shook his head and, I swear, made a *tsk, tsk* sound.

I needed him to stay focused. "Milo, why do you say Ambrose has a short temper?"

"He was flailing his arms around, his face was beet red—like almost purple—and I swear fire was going to burst out of his ears at any moment."

I filed that image away with a reminder to learn how elemental witches summoned their power. "Could you hear what he was yelling about?"

"Of course I could. Once it all started, I slipped around the protection spell and sat near Ambrose, who was demanding access to the scene. He said he wanted to look for clues."

"I'm assuming Jessie refused."

"He did, but that Ambrose fella wasn't having any of it and, finally, Shepard had the sense to calm him down with a bit of magic."

"What? Jessie used magic on a suspect?" I paced in a small circle in the kitchen. "That's not how we do things. Could it taint the investigation if Ambrose had been under the influence of magic?"

"Relax, my dear witch. It was a minor de-escalation spell. Just enough to take the edge off his anger. Which, for the record, is understandable; after all, his sister was murdered."

I tore off several slices of Milo's favorite smoked salmon. Brutus lumbered into the kitchen and stared at Milo. He drooled. I handed him a hunk, too.

"Hey, that's my special treat." Milo took a swipe at Brutus. "He has those dry cookies in the closet. Give him those."

I returned the package to the fridge. "In this family, we share everything."

"Great, you're marrying Detective Cutie, and he adopts this lug, and I'm stuck with both."

"Stop your grousing. You love Gage, and Brutus has grown on you."

"Not that much." He hopped down, took another swipe over Brutus's nose but didn't make contact, and trotted from the room.

I rubbed Brutus's head and kissed the spot between his ears. "Don't listen to Milo. In his way, he's glad you're here."

Brutus gave a deep woof and ambled down the hall in the same direction Milo took.

I waved a hand toward the pantry, and my clue board slid out and opened. I grinned. "There are perks to being a witch."

Nikki giggled. "I seem to recall when you first discovered you had magic, you said you wanted to do things the non-magical way, including washing dishes. Now look at you. Moving objects took me a lot longer to master."

"Thanks for the vote of confidence." I took the marker and wrote—stabbed in the neck, beside Shula's name.

I tapped the marker on the board. "What else do we know about the crime?

Nikki said, "The timeline doesn't add up. Shula texted her brother at two and was nervous about something. Violet said they were gone thirty minutes before they returned; however, that was after we arrived. That doesn't compute since Ravena said they left at two. We arrived around three-fifteen, but they weren't here, and based on her text to Ambrose, Shula had been alone long before two, which is in direct conflict with Ravena and Violet or Morgaine's statement."

I jotted down the notes. "Let's guess they left Shula around one-thirty, which would give her time to get the heebie-jeebies. The three witches were gone for almost two hours when they finally returned. And they went to the beach. Could one of them have circled back, killed Shula, and gotten back to the shore without the other two's knowledge?"

"They only had one car."

"But they are witches, and Ravena is an air witch, right?"

"Why do you think that?"

"Erikson. It has air right in the name and supports our belief that the elements are tied to their last names." I snapped my fingers. "I need to call Glinda and see if she knows anything about these four families. If Ravena is a distant relation to Gage and she's an air witch, could she have used her power to manipulate the air currents to get her here and back without anyone noticing she was gone?" I picked up my cell and waited for Glinda to answer.

Chapter 8
Lily

"Hi, Glinda, it's Lily."

"Hello, Lily. This is a lovely surprise. I thought you and Nikki were having a girls' day. Mindy and I got everything done, if you're calling to see how the to-do is coming." The warmth of her voice spilled over as if she were standing in front of me, smiling.

"We were, and that's great news about the list. Sadly, there was an incident, and I wanted to ask for your help."

"Anything." Her voice hadn't changed, but I could sense her curiosity.

"A woman has been murdered across the street from my house. Shula Ashton, from Pine Valley."

"That's awful. I don't know her personally, but I've heard the name." The way she drew out her response made me perk up. Did she know more than she was saying?

"What about Ravena Erikson? Do you know if her family is related to Burke?"

"Gage and his dad aren't related to that branch of the Erikson family tree. That family are air witches."

I wanted to ask if she was sure since Ravena had claimed Gage was a cousin of some sort.

"It's a coincidence, nothing more. What happened to the Ashton woman?"

"She was stabbed in the neck with a piece of wood. The autopsy report will provide more specifics, but it's a tragedy."

"It is." She paused and cleared her throat.

"Does Gage think you're in danger staying at the house?"

"No. I've got Brutus and Milo, and I'll enhance my protection charms as soon as I can."

"Lily, do you know what kind of wood was used?"

"Hm. It was dark, like mahogany. Is that important?"

"It's a question you should ask EL. If it's yew or elder wood, both can be used with bad intentions, and this would certainly apply. But now that I think of it, the elder is pale in color. If I had to guess, it would be yew, and some witches believe it holds the power of life or death."

A shiver raced over my arms, and my heart thumped quicker. "Which would mean someone could have chosen that wood for that purpose."

"Likely to be the case. Is there anything else I can answer?"

"What about nymphs and fairies?"

"They live near Pine Valley, too."

I knew but didn't want to come off as rude, so I said, "Do you think they're friendly with the elemental witches?" I couldn't help but shake the feeling that I saw someone in the woods after I discovered Shula dead.

"Possibly. Are you asking if they practice magic together?"

"Yes. I should be more direct. This may seem odd, but I thought I saw someone moving along the tree line when I discovered Shula. Never mind my rambling. It must have been the breeze or a trick of light."

"Typically, fairies and nymphs don't practice magic with anyone. They're considered a positive magical force and elemental witches, and some full witches, are known to be temperamental and not good at working together."

"Really, but when we were putting the haunted house on for the town, lots of witches from the coven worked with us to make it a memorable event."

Glinda laughed softly, "Except for the first night, when you discovered a dead clown. And the second attempt to hold the haunted house, you found yourself in a tight spot."

That was an understatement. My rib cage felt too tight as I took a deep breath, trying to push away the memory of being the target. "But that wasn't a witch intent on causing harm, just a criminal."

"Please be careful. With everything happening right now, the wedding and these witches showing up out of the blue, you need to remain vigilant."

"I will. Thanks, Glinda." After I hung up, I realized I had never acknowledged that I knew about the upcoming change to the coven. There would be time for that after the wedding.

Nikki and I finished setting the table for supper. It could accommodate ten people if Aunt Mimi and Nate came, but I doubted it since her focus would be on magic, and half the people at dinner were non-magical and didn't know witches existed.

"I don't remember asking Gage to pick up takeout." My skills in the kitchen were lacking. I could make breakfast, but I was doubtful I could whip up something that resembled a decent dinner for eight or more people. I went to the freezer, hoping there was still a pan of lasagna in there.

"Relax." Nikki said, "I've got it covered." The oven timer dinged, and she opened the door. "Enchiladas, and in the fridge, I have an avocado and fresh corn salad chilling and flan for dessert."

"Oh good." I gave her a wink. "Care to accompany me to the crime scene?"

"I thought you told Gage we would go as a group?"

"I did, but with just the two of us, we can see if there's a magic signature or something other than what non-magicals can see."

She took a step in my direction and held out her hand. "On one condition: we should be extra careful."

"Why does everyone keep saying be careful? This isn't our first crime scene."

She shook her head. "No, but you're getting married in a few days, and cuts, bruises, or worse need to be avoided at all costs."

Raising my voice, I said, "How about we bring Milo with us? He can keep an eye out." I tipped my head to the hall, waited, touched my ear, and grinned. I heard tiny claws clicking against the wood floor.

"Did I hear my name?" Milo grumbled.

"We're going across the street. Do you want to go with us and keep a sharp eye on things while we poke around?"

"Mimi added the enhanced spell on that area, and Jonesy and Shepard are still hovering. Do you think they'll allow you to get close enough to check out the scene?"

"Yes." I picked him up. "Are you saying you want to accompany us or stay where it's climate controlled?"

"Fine. But I'm going under a slight protest,

and I will get another chunk of smoked salmon for this."

I kissed his little head. "Agreed."

Placing him gently on the floor, Nikki opened the back door, and he scampered ahead of us.

I gave her a saucy wink. "That was easy."

She giggled. "You're good."

We jogged across the street, and Jessie strode over. "Lily, Nikki. What's up?"

Without looking around, I gestured to the crime scene tape. "We're going to take a walk around the perimeter. I thought I saw something earlier and want to check it out."

"We've combed the area, and nothing seems out of place."

"Well, there are a couple of things bothering me. One that strikes me as odd is our victim didn't have a purse with her, and the other is that I'm sure I saw something or someone in the tree line; so, to satisfy my curiosity, I thought I'd look around."

"Suit yourself. If you need me or Jonesy, holler."

"Thanks, Jessie." Nikki and I walked in the grassy area along the tree line with our heads down.

"I didn't realize you saw something in the trees earlier. You didn't mention it."

I shrugged. "Initially, I thought it was no big deal. But it's gnawing at me, almost like I've missed an important clue."

So far, nothing had been overlooked. Not that I expected it, with our police officers and detectives on the scene, but there was a slim chance we could find something. We walked up and down several times, scuffing the grassy area. If Jonesy hadn't been watching us, I would have magicked a rake and used it to see if there was a clue. When that yielded nothing, I pointed to the line of trees.

"I'm going to walk on the other side."

Nikki nodded. "Let's mirror each other, and I'll walk on this side." She handed me a flashlight. "This might help."

Jonesy had his back to us when I glanced his way.

Nikki smiled. "No worries, he wasn't watching us."

"You're pretty smart."

She tapped her brow. "Just call me Dr. Watson."

I looked from left to right. "We should start about twenty feet in either direction of the actual scene. If I had been someone trying to sneak up on an unsuspecting person, I would have ducked into the trees."

Nikki's brow furrowed. "Which way do you think she was looking?"

I closed my eyes briefly, remembering how her body was found. "She was looking at the house. It would have been easy for someone to sneak up behind her and lash out."

We paced the length of the tree line. "Lily, do you have any idea what the motive would have been?"

"Not yet. Her friends indicated they all wanted to talk to me. Ambrose wasn't much help, either—other than Shula was uncomfortable after the others left her."

"Do you think she was anxious about talking to you?"

"Why? It's not like we had a history; let's be honest, I'll be brand new to my role within the coven. I have zero clout in any matter. Besides, it's a democracy."

"That's not true. As the most powerful witch, you wield much clout. However, I'm curious what happened all those years ago."

We walked a few more paces in silence. "Do you think my book could shed some light on the history of what happened between the elemental witches and full-blood witches? The spells have been passed down for generations. Maybe it will if I'm looking for answers with pure intent."

"It can't hurt to view it with a curious mind. You've always said it shows what you need to know when you need to know it."

"Yeah, and I need to understand much more than just the fracture between the two groups. Like how, as a Michaels witch, am I going to take over for Mimi when there's so much I can't do." We were well past the crime scene, and the tree line had grown dense. My steps slowed. "Hello? What do we have here." I knelt on the pine needles and the smell of spruce wafted up.

"Did you find something?"

I withdrew a pair of latex gloves from my pocket and slipped them on. Brushing the needles aside, I saw a narrow sheath of leather. Something that reminded me of what a knife could be kept in. "Look. Someone needs to take pictures and bag this as evidence."

"Do you think the killer dropped it?"

"By looking at the leather, it hasn't been out here long. This could be an important clue. I'll wait here. Can you get one of the officers to come over and catalog this?"

"Sure." Nikki zipped back in the direction we came.

I rocked back on my heels and closed my eyes. A slight tremor of magic pulsed in the air.

I needed to see if I could capture the essence to examine later. "There's magic in the air. I care to know who left it there. The discovery will provide direction to solve, the mystery that will protect us all. For this I wish, so it shall be."

A silver shimmer appeared before me. I held open my hand. When it rested in my palm, I turned my latex glove inside out to keep it contained.

Milo trotted over. "My dear witch, what do you have there?"

"Milo," I dropped my voice so it wouldn't carry. "I did a spell to pull residual magic into the palm of my hand, and then I wrapped my glove around it. But now I don't know what to do with it. It's not like I want Jonesy to see it and wonder if the stress of the wedding has me not thinking clearly."

"First, no one would ever think that. You're too sharp." He narrowed his eyes. "Maybe you might succumb to stress for our upcoming wedding."

My brow cocked. "Our wedding?"

"Of course, you're marrying Detective Cutie, and we're becoming a family. So, it's our wedding."

I saw his point, and my heart softened. He did like Gage. "Quick, picture the glove on the back deck inside that pot of basil you're trying to grow."

"Why there?"

"Basil plants are known to protect. You can't have unknown magic in your house. It's not safe. But sitting in the pot, it will be perfectly safe."

In my mind's eye, I pictured the oddly tied glove tucked among the plant's stems. "Rest in safety until it's time to reveal the truth left behind. For this I wish, so it shall be."

"Well done, Lily. You have come a long way in discovering your power."

With Milo's compliment, I pulled my shoulders back and tilted my chin up. "Thank you for your vote of confidence."

Milo's tail sliced through the air. "Let's face it. If you fall flat on your face when you do, you know, the coven thing, it's a reflection that I've failed as a familiar and teacher. We can't let that happen."

I shook my head slowly. "Milo" Before I could say anything else, I heard Gage's voice blend with Nikki's. I stayed where I was, and Milo slipped into the shadows.

She glanced from side to side. "I thought Milo was here?"

"No, he's not." I stood as Gage held out his hand to me. Glancing behind them, I was relieved there was still time to speak freely. "The residual magic has been secured for Aunt Mimi to examine later."

Nikki's brows shot to her hairline. "The what?"

"You heard me." I inclined my head in the direction of Sharon and Mac. "Later."

Sharon scanned the area. "Lily, what made you come this far down the tree line?"

"I remember what Ambrose said about Shula trying to reach him and that she was unnerved. I wondered if someone had been watching the four women and waited for the opportune moment to attack."

Mac whipped out an evidence bag. "Peabody, you've got the camera?"

She held it up and began to take a series of pictures from many angles. "You didn't find anything else?"

Nikki cleared her throat. Sharon gave her a sharp look and then turned to face me. "Lily?"

"This was the only piece of tangible evidence we discovered."

Gage said, "It might help to figure out who else was here. With some luck, maybe we'll be able to get a print of it, too."

"That's expecting a lot, but we'll do our best." Snapping on gloves, Sharon picked up the sheath and slipped it into Mac's bag. "We'll run this to the station and secure it for the night. Tomorrow, we can dust for fingerprints."

Mac said, "Boss, we can do it tonight if you'd rather?"

Sharon popped her hand on her hip. "And miss Lily's clue board? Not a chance."

Gage tucked a lock of hair behind my ear. "I think your board is becoming legendary."

"I wouldn't go that far. I think it's all that brain power in one room and, of course," I grinned at Nikki. "Good food doesn't hurt, either."

Chapter 9
Gage

Sitting around Lily's kitchen table, I realized this would be one of the last times I'd refer to it as hers; soon, it would be ours. Having our friends, who were like family, join us was even better. Despite the reason we were gathered around the table, it warmed my soul.

A tap on the kitchen door drew my attention. Mimi and Nate strode in. "Hello, everyone." Her eyes sought Lily's. "Dear, would you join me on the deck?" She gave me a sweet smile. "Bride to auntie chat."

She wasn't fooling me. It was about the glove of residual magic securely tucked into the planter on the deck. Lily followed her outside and closed the door. I was sure a silencing spell was added, too, to make sure the non-magicals didn't hear about the glove.

"Nate, take a seat. We're getting ready for dessert."

He pulled out a chair. "Don't mind if I do."

Steve passed him a plate and fork. "My bride whipped up a delicious flan."

Nate rubbed his hands together. "My favorite." He looked around the group. "How's the investigation going?"

Mac and Peabody shot me a questioning look with brows arched and heads tipped to one side.

I bobbed my head in Nate's direction. "Mimi would have told Nate what happened here. Since he was in town, he might have seen something."

Mac turned in his chair to face him. "Currently, there's not much to go on. There are no witnesses to anyone loitering; the three women claim they were at the beach. We've already checked, and the car was in the parking lot near the comfort center. The victim's brother was in Pine Valley and EL's estimated the time of death. Other than the implement used, we're at a standstill."

"Time of death was around two?" Nate looked at EL.

"Between two and two-fifteen." He clasped his hands in his lap. "Are you familiar with different types of woods?"

Nate lifted his spoon and tasted the flan. He paused while his eyes fluttered shut. "Steve, you're one lucky guy. This flan is perfection." He glanced over his shoulder to the door and then winked at Steve. "But don't tell my wife that."

Steve beamed. "My lips are sealed."

"EL, I've seen a lot in my day as the captain of a lobster boat how a shard of wood can become a dangerous weapon." He continued to savor his flan.

"Do you know how a shard of wood can be hardened other than by nature petrifying it?" EL leaned forward, his focus on Nate.

"There are a lot of different methods. Epoxy-based polymers are one idea that springs to mind." He gave EL an assessing look. "I'm guessing this wasn't a shard of wood picked up from the ground and used?"

EL shook his head. "No. This was not a method of convenience. It was filed to a point, and the wood had been hardened. Someone knew what they were doing."

I hadn't thought of that. Would an earth witch be familiar with trees and the wood from them to know which were the strongest?

Lily stuck her head around the kitchen door. "EL, would you join us for a moment?"

I wanted to ask if I could come, too, but since I had learned that EL was a witch and not only our coroner, it made sense that Lily would want him to be informed about the residual magic.

He pushed back from the table and touched Sharon's hand. "I'll be right back."

"I'll come with you." She moved to stand. He said, "Stay and ask Nate a few more questions."

Giving him a thoughtful look, she settled into her chair. "You'll tell me if this is important to the case?"

He kissed the top of her head. "Of course I will."

But if the topic involved magic, he would have to keep it to himself. As far as I knew, Sharon and Mac still had no clue about the witches who lived in our community. I'm not sure I was comfortable with them being clueless. Especially when crimes involved magic. I struggled with how I could protect them from bad actors.

She shot me a look, and I shrugged. "If Lily wanted me, she would have asked. Or she would have come in and talked to all of us."

Nikki said, "Who'd like more coffee or tea?"

We made eye contact and I mouthed,

"Thank you." Hot beverages were always a good diversion.

"I'll get it." Sharon went to the counter.

Nikki followed her.

Nate finished his flan and set his spoon on the table. "You know, I've been sitting here thinking about this poor girl being left all alone on the side of the road." He looked at me. "This is a safe neighborhood, so there's no way this was a crime of opportunity. She was targeted. Someone waited until she was alone."

"We all agree with that. Stabbing is personal since you're close to the victim."

"Could the three women have been in it together? They pretend to leave, park their car in that lot, circle back through the woods, sneak up behind her, and bam. Plunging the wooden stake into her neck is more like killing a vampire than a human. They'd also have to know something about anatomy to make sure a sharpened piece of wood caused enough damage to kill her."

"Maybe they didn't intend for her to die but

just injure her. Hitting the carotid might have been pure chance."

He gave a thoughtful nod. "EL should weigh in on this conversation." He smiled at Nikki as she placed a mug of coffee on the table before him. "Mighty fine flan, young lady."

"There's more." She winked at him. "I won't tell Mimi should you want to indulge."

He patted his midsection. "Better not. There's going to be enough good food at the wedding this weekend. But thank you."

The kitchen door opened. EL entered with Lily and Mimi behind him. Their faces were drawn tight, and my stomach churned. Whatever they'd discovered couldn't be discussed now, but Lily would fill me in later.

"EL." Nate pulled out the vacant chair beside him and gestured for him to sit. "I was sharing my thoughts about the case." He held up his hand as EL glanced at me. "I know you're thinking I'm a lobster man, not a lawman, but sometimes answering a layperson's questions can help clarify a few things."

"Lay it on me." EL gave Nate his undivided attention.

"Do you think hitting the carotid artery was by accident? And how much force would be needed to do the deed with the weapon of choice?"

"I can't give away specifics, but I think the killer got lucky by hitting the artery. I don't mean that to be flippant. It would be difficult with a single stab to puncture it as precisely as it happened. Regarding the weapon, whoever fashioned it made sure the length of the blade was razor sharp. Now, from the angle of the injury, the attacker was right-handed and came from behind. They must have been in a rage based on the wound's depth. In addition, I believe they had an altercation with the victim at some point."

Lily stepped in front of the board. "Why do you say that?"

With a half nod, I encouraged EL to continue talking. There was so much that wouldn't be shared about this conversation with the department's higher-ups. What was another trusted person to be brought in to help?

"Adrenaline is fueled by rage. The attacker moved fast and jabbed hard and deep. Unless they were superhuman, it's the only explanation."

Or magical? But the guiding principle of magical people I'd met over the years is to *do no harm*.

Lily crossed her arms over her midsection and tapped her foot while looking at the ceiling. "All right. Let's suppose Shula had an argument with someone, she knew her attacker. I need to talk to Ambrose. He thinks it's one of the three women, but he'd know if someone else had been arguing with his sister." She closed her eyes. "I didn't want to say anything, and I'm not sure if I saw what I thought I saw. But when I discovered Shula's body, I saw movement in the tree line. It was just a flash and then it was gone. I chalked it up to a trick of the light or breeze at the time but I'm not sure anymore. Especially since EL described the attack; that would have been the same general direction. You know, to attack."

Sharon took a few steps from the counter closer to the clue board. "What exactly did you see, Lily?"

"That's all. Just a flash. You know, like in a dream where it's so fleeting you're unsure if you even had a dream. Or maybe it's more like looking through dense fog."

"We should do another sweep of the area." She gave Mac a head bob in the direction of the door.

"Nikki and I looked. That's how we found the leather sheath."

"We can search again in the morning. I don't think anything will change overnight. The scene is sealed off, and Lily and I made sure the security cameras on the house cover it. If anyone were to come back, we'll have them on video and, of course, Brutus will send up an alarm."

Sharon balled her hands at her sides. "All this waiting around is frustrating."

"We all feel the same." I pointed to Lily's clue board. "What else should we talk about?"

She scanned the few details listed and grimaced. "We don't seem to have anything new. Without talking to Ambrose, looking at the scene again and—" Lily turned away and sniffled.

I hurried over and wrapped my arms around her from the back. "Hey. We'll find out who did this."

She sniffled again. "I'm going outside for a minute." She slipped from my arms and hurried out the back door.

"Hey, everyone. Do you mind if we call it a night? Lily's been working hard on the wedding plans, and today added a whole new level of stress." On top of whatever it was she hadn't been able to tell me yet.

Mac got up. "I should be getting home anyway. Margaret texted a while ago saying she'd finally gotten Amanda down for the night."

I clapped him on the shoulder. "I hope the baby's feeling much better in the morning."

"Thanks, Gage. If you need anything tonight, don't hesitate to call." He walked toward the front door. I appreciated that he gave Lily space.

EL and Sharon were right behind him. "I'll have the full report for you in the morning." Sharon took his hand. "With skill and a healthy dose of luck, maybe we can wrap this up fast."

She glanced over her shoulder. "Tell Lily goodnight for us."

I leaned against the door after I closed it and took several deep breaths. I've never seen Lily brought to tears because of a case, except when I got kidnapped. This was different.

Nikki stepped around the corner. "Gage, are you coming?"

I rolled my shoulders. "Right behind you."

Mimi and Nate were at the table. She gestured to my chair. "Have a seat."

I looked at the door.

"She needs a few minutes." Mimi patted the seat cushion.

I wanted to stand but ignoring her would have been rude.

Steve poured me another cup of coffee. Nikki sat beside him as we waited for Lily to come inside.

Milo trotted through the kitchen and slipped out his kitty door.

The air was heavy and tension gripped my body. I drank coffee to keep my hands busy.

The door eased open. Lily entered, carrying Milo in her arms. Her cheeks were sunken, and her sable-brown eyes were wide. I moved to stand but she shook her head.

"Don't get up." She slipped into the chair next to me and took my hand. Milo remained in her lap, purring. I was sure he was comforting her. I felt my throat growing tight as I gave her my full attention.

"Lily. What's wrong? I know you're more upset than because of the—" I jerked my thumb in the direction of the crime scene.

She gave me a sorrow-filled smile. "This has less to do with the murder and more how our future is about to change. Even that's tied to the murder. I can't put all the pieces together, at least not yet."

I squeezed her hand. "You're starting to ramble."

Her gaze went to Milo. He purred again. "I know. But what if—"

He purred even louder and tapped his paw against her cheek. My heart constricted seeing her familiar giving her comfort, which I would have been doing if I knew what the heck was going on.

"Let's talk about the easy stuff first." She tipped her head in Nikki's direction. "Thanks for not getting your wand shaking when I didn't ask you to join us on the deck. EL needed to see what we discovered since it could help him with the autopsy."

"I never let stuff like that bother me. You'll fill me in when you can."

"Gage, earlier, we discovered some residual magic where we found the sheath; I firmly believe it held the dagger used to kill Shula. I secured the magic and stored it in the basil plant, which protected everyone until we knew what we were up against."

"What did you learn about the magic?"

Aunt Mimi cleared her throat. "The spell is ancient, and the user hasn't performed much magic in a long time. They were a bit rusty."

"How can you tell?" I looked at Mimi and then Lily and back to Mimi.

"Magic is like sound waves. These were weaker than they should have been. I believe the dagger will have the same residual magic, which is why we need EL to examine it carefully."

"At least we know they're connected. Is there a way to track it back to an individual?"

Mimi shook her head. "Not yet, but there could be." Her gaze landed on Lily.

"What am I missing?" I felt like a ping-pong ball bouncing between the two women.

"Remember, we talked about me taking over as head of the coven? After our wedding, when Aunt Mimi steps down as head of the

Pembroke Cove Witches Coven and I assume the role, I will be faced with the decision to hear the elemental witches' petition to rejoin the coven."

I didn't say a word. My mind raced with worst-case scenarios, but I wasn't even sure what they might be. Could the coven run amok? Would more witches in town become problematic? Ancient spells? I slumped against the back of the chair, and my mouth gaped open. "What's next?"

Chapter 10
Lily

I squeezed Gage's hand as every ounce of color drained from his face. Milo grumbled. "I told you he wouldn't handle the news well once it sunk in what was about to happen." He jumped into Gage's lap and lay his head on Gage's chest. For a change, he was purring in a soft, comforting tone.

Gage ran a hand down his back as he blinked rapidly. There might have been a better way to discuss the recent events, but I just ripped the bandage off since one event must be tied to the other.

Everyone around the table held their comments.

When I caught Nikki's soft, round eyes, she placed her hand over her heart.

I felt terrible for Gage. This was a lot to absorb, but he was up to the task.

"Lily, I know you told me but with the on-going investigation I didn't take it all in." He shifted in the chair and continued to stroke Milo's back. "As head of the coven, your first challenge will be a problem that has been lingering for decades?"

I nodded, giving him time to formulate his follow-up questions.

Milo grumbled. "Gentle with the familiar, DC." He squirmed in Gage's lap and dropped to the floor with a thud. "That's what happens when you try to support a non-magical." He trotted to where Brutus had taken his usual spot at the door. "Move over, you big lug." He curled between the dog's front legs and placed his head on one.

Mimi said, "Gage, Lily never read the

coven charter. Those that had, knew a powerful Michaels witch would face this challenge."

"She's a new witch. I know what you and Nikki said. I still don't understand how her powers could be stronger than yours. It's illogical. You've been a witch your entire life." He glanced my way and shrugged his shoulders. "No offense, sweetheart."

"I said the same thing, but there's that little caveat about your mother's magic. The magic of a powerful Erikson witch will combine with my magic to give me a boost."

Mimi's pride showed in her eyes. "Not that she needs it. I've seen what Lily can do with little effort. Her intention is strong, and she can cast a spell in her own words like no witch I've ever seen before, including me."

"Thanks, Aunt Mimi. That's not really true, but sweet nonetheless." I didn't want anyone to think I was being a show-off or that this news had gone to my head. Inside, I was terrified, thinking I was about to commit the biggest mistakes a witch could make in the history of witches. I took a slow, deep breath to soothe my thoughts, which were threatening to run away.

Nikki reached across the table and touched his arm. "Gage, Lily isn't in this alone. As her oldest and best friend, I will have a spot on the council, the witch version of Sherlock Holmes and Dr. Watson. In addition, Jessie and EL will be elevated within the coven."

He turned in the chair, grabbed my hands, and pulled me into his lap. "Is this what you want?" He brushed a lock of hair from my cheek.

I tipped my chin up slightly. "I'm a Michaels witch. If it's my destiny to oversee the council for all my natural days, then I will. As for the elementals, I'll face that head-on."

Aunt Mimi's smile grew wider. "She's going to be amazing. Her kindness, compassion, and empathy make her a natural fit, and that she's lived as a non-magical person for most of her life is an asset in her new role."

He looked at Aunt Mimi and Nikki, sitting

at our kitchen table. "You'll stand beside her? I couldn't bear it if anything happened to her."

"Nothing will, Gage. In some ways, she's more protected. Every witch in the coven is excited about the change. They've watched her become a fine witch over the last few years."

"How is she more protected?" His gaze was locked on my aunt.

"Well, with other magical beings coming to town, like what's happened now, it would be forbidden to show up at Lily's doorstep looking to plead their case."

He nodded. "That's good." Saying the right words was one thing, but the tone of his voice told me he wasn't convinced. "How will they not be able to find us?"

"The house will be cloaked from magicals not belonging to the coven. To everyone, this house will be a home. In addition, Lily and you will increase the protection spells."

"I'm not a witch."

"Magic is in the intention. You will draw on your mother's magic and the love you share to work the spell with Lily to increase the protection for your family."

He shook his head. "I'm confused; then I'll be a witch, too?"

"No." Aunt Mimi sighed. "Think of it more like muscle memory. You inherited genes from both parents. Although your magic is non-existent, your mother's magic is dormant in you. When you and Lily combine your intention to protect your home, the magic will come forth. But it won't change who you are. Does that make sense?"

He nodded, his face expressionless, and I wasn't sure what he was thinking.

My heart thundered in my chest. "Do you want to postpone our marriage? I know this is a lot to take in, and I'm glad we found out before the wedding. Could you imagine if we discovered this after? Then you'd be trapped, and I'd never want to do anything like that to you. So, if you want to change your mind, tell me, and we'll call the whole thing off. Aunt Mimi will continue to oversee the coven."

He grinned. "Are you going to take a breath or just keep talking?"

My breath shuddered in and out. I froze, even though I wanted to run out the back door and give him a chance to decide what he wanted for his future without me pressuring him.

Cupping my cheeks in his hands, he kissed me lightly. "I've waited my entire adult life to marry you. Nothing will change that, not even if your skin goes green and you get a huge wart on the end of your nose."

"That's not real..."

He kissed me again mid-sentence and laughed. "What I mean is: nothing is going to change my mind. I love you and we are getting married. Head of the coven, murder victims, or a major crime spree—it's you and me against the world."

I felt a rush of warmth from my toes to my face. "You're sure."

"I'm as sure about marrying you as we are

about the sun rising in the east." He kissed me again.

Steve said, "Hey, enough of the mushy stuff. Can we get back to part two of the news? The Pine Valley contingent."

I watched as Gage's eyes switched from tender to serious. "Steve's right. We must talk about Shula Ashton and our next steps."

Aunt Mimi said, "Tea and cookies are in order before we discuss Pine Valley." With a wave of her hand, she reset the table with cups, several pots of tea, and an overflowing plate of cookies.

Slipping into the chair next to me, we sat, holding hands under the table.

She cleared her throat. "We'll start with the basics of elemental witches and why they're not part of the coven. But to be clear, this event happened decades ago, and we must remember we shouldn't hold the sins of the ancestors against the children. In this case, Pine Valley's current witch community members deserve to be heard."

"Aunt Mimi, that's a great statement. Why are they coming back now? Do they think I'm an easy mark?"

"Probably because I've been head of the council since I was twenty. Comparatively, it had only been a short time since the incident, and no one was ready for a change."

Nikki nodded. "I remember my grandmother telling me stories about a group of witches who wanted to use their powers for mischief and mayhem against non-magicals."

"Were they evil?" My mouth went dry. What was I about to come up against? I've had one scary run-in with an evil witch and a few off their brooms, but confronting an entire group was frightening.

"No, when elemental witches work together, their powers are extreme. For example, they could instantly wipe out a farmer's crop. Like setting fire to it, the wind whips the fire into a frenzy, floods it with water, and then heals the land again." She held up her finger. "If they were so inclined to do so."

"That's awful. If they were doing that stuff, I can see why they'd be voted out of the coven." Nikki's face was ashen. "Imagine all the people that would hurt. Not just the farmer but the people who relied on his crops for food."

Aunt Mimi picked up her teacup and sipped. "Again, I said that was an extreme example; but at the time, the council was concerned things would escalate, and they didn't want that in Pembroke Cove. There was a vote and anyone who wanted to live that type of magical life was asked to leave our town."

"All the elemental witches moved to Pine Valley?" I knew more information was better to help with our case.

Nikki passed her the cookie plate. She waved it away. "Not at first. They weren't sure where they were moving. The nymphs and fairies had created a tight-knit community there. They didn't want trouble. However, being a kind and soft-hearted group, they eventually agreed with a strict set of guidelines in place. Any magic combined with another's to cause harm would not be tolerated. Do you see the difference? They could do magic together; our coven wouldn't allow that since it had already gone too far."

Gage said, "How does this relate to today?"

My aunt said, "Two things spring to mind. They're sincere and want to rejoin or think Lily will be a pushover so they can hoodwink her into supporting their cause."

I snorted. "If they think the second part, they have another thing coming. I have a sixth sense when people are lying."

Gage squeezed my hand. "Ain't that the truth? If they're looking for acceptance, why would Shula have been murdered?"

Nate clasped his hands on the table. "If you're interested in my thoughts, someone is sending a message to indicate that the Pine Valley witches haven't changed and shouldn't be trusted. Killing one of their own is in direct violation of how our witches live their lives. Do no harm."

Steve said, "So if one of the elemental

witches is murdered, it will cast a long shadow of doubt over the rest."

Aunt Mimi nodded. "Honestly, that's what it's done for me. I'm sure it will do the same for the rest of the coven council once the news is out."

I pushed back from the table and walked to my clue board. "Where does that leave us, and how do we bring Sharon and Mac into the investigation? They don't have any idea that witches exist in our town. You can't explain a rift in the two towns without explaining the basic problem."

Gage said, "Then we treat it like a regular crime to everyone but the people in this room and EL."

"Tomorrow, Nikki and I will go to Pine Valley to see what we can discover from the witch angle. Gage, you and the police department will work the crime scene again and look for additional clues. Aunt Mimi, at some point in the morning, can you double-check to see if anyone tried to weaken your barrier around the crime scene? That will give us a good starting point. We'll meet here for lunch to share what we learn."

Nate said, "I'll man the bookstore until my mermaid arrives."

I blew him a kiss. "You're a good uncle." I looked around the table, and my gaze stopped at Gage. He gave me a wink. "You got this covered."

I stood a little straighter. "With the right people working together, there isn't anything we can't accomplish."

"Where do we go from here?" Nikki asked. "Do you have a theory yet?"

"If someone decided to kill Shula Ashton so that she couldn't talk to me, why not attempt to stop all of the women? This means there's another reason why Shula was silenced. Stabbing is an up close and personal act. Someone hated her. We heard what EL said; it was luck that the shard of wood punctured her artery, especially since the angle of the wound indicated that the attacker had come from behind. Whoever it was wanted to inflict a grave injury, maybe as a warning. Death may not have been the motivation."

"Mimi, have you heard anything about the Pine Valley witches seeking out Lily once she's appointed head of the council? There must have been rumors."

"Gage, that's an excellent point. We haven't heard a thing. Which, in and of itself, is odd. With any major transition, you would think some of the Pine Valley witches would have conversations with members of our coven. That's something I can check into in the morning. If anyone's been approached, I'll be able to find out."

"Excellent. I'll see you here tomorrow?"

She nodded. "Yes, after you and the other police officers have rechecked the area, I'll confirm if anyone tried to get past my spell magically."

Nate said, "Before I open the bookstore, I can ask if anyone noticed the women who claim to have been at the beach. We know the car was there, but there's nothing corroborating their statement that they stayed at the beach. Late in August, more locals are enjoying the shore than vacationers. Someone at the marina might have noticed them on the beach, especially with that one, Morgaine, being drawn to the water."

I gave him a sharp look. "We never said that she went in the ocean."

He gave me an indulgent smile. "Lily, she's a water witch. I've been around a long time and seen a few things running a lobster boat over the years. She'd be like a duck, unable to resist going in."

"Good point. Thanks for volunteering to poke around."

Gage leaned forward, his arms resting on the table. "Nate, that's something the police should do."

He gave Gage the same smile as he'd given to me. "Some folks won't share what they know with anyone except a crusty old dude with sea-water in his veins. Trust me on this one. If there's something to find, I will."

Mimi said, "Gage, I know it's hard to let civilians into your case, but in this family, we help each other, and the sooner we can clear up this murder mess, the happier a wedding day you and my niece will have. If anyone deserves their happily ever after it's the two of you."

Steve tapped the tabletop. "Gage, if it makes you feel any better, I don't have anyone to question but I'll keep my eyes open for anything unusual."

I couldn't help but laugh. "Well played, my friend."

Chapter 11
Lily

Seven-thirty on the dot, Nikki sailed in the back door. She held to-go coffee cups and carried a floral tin. My mouth began to water. "Cookies?"

"Better. Breakfast sandwiches made with small waffles."

Milo trotted into the kitchen. "Did I hear someone mention breakfast?"

I put my hand on my hip. "You've had breakfast—an entire can of tuna and a bowl of kitty milk."

"Never underestimate your familiar. I have

room for a second breakfast." He sat back on his haunches and stared at the tin.

Laughing, I bent down and kissed his head. "You can't magic it open."

"No. But I can try." He tipped his head. "Where are you witches off to bright and early? Wedding preparations?"

"Nope. I called Mom when I got up and asked if she and Glinda could get together again, review the to-do list, and ensure all is ready for the wedding. Glinda said it was complete, but I'd feel better with one final check. Which reminds me, what happened to your bowtie? I didn't see it on my dresser."

"I don't want to wear a green one, as it will clash with my eyes. I prefer black to match Detective Cutie's tux."

I glanced at Nikki, who held her hand over her mouth, but I could see laughter hovering in her eyes. "Since when did you get concerned about the color of a bowtie?"

"Since I'm going to be standing in front of all these people, witches and non-magicals. I need to look my best." He dipped his head. "Of course, I won't outshine the bride and groom, which reminds me: Brutus should be at the wedding, too, and he'll need a bowtie to match mine."

I crossed my arms over my tummy to not chuckle out loud. "Really?"

"We discussed it. Well, it was more of a familiar-to-dog conversation, but we agreed that if we were going to be a family, we should start off on the right paw."

"I'll make sure to get you and Brutus matching bowties."

"We've got that ticked off your to-do list. Are we going sleuthing today?"

I picked up my shoulder bag and keys. "Nikki and I are going to Pine Valley, but I need you to stay here and watch the crime scene. I want to poke around and see if anyone mentions they were with the women."

"Oh, there were a couple of nymphs and even a fairy hanging around for a while. They had a heated exchange with the ladies, including the victim." He swished his tail and took a step toward the other room.

I snapped my fingers. "Freeze, mister."

He looked over his shoulder. "What? Change your mind about my second breakfast?"

"No." I threw my hands up in the air. "Why didn't you tell me there were other people outside, other than the four women?"

"You didn't ask, and I didn't see how it was relevant. After the argument, they said they were leaving. However, since you mentioned you saw someone in the trees, I'm guessing either they stayed as a group or left one behind." He jerked his tail back and forth, slicing it through the air. "Wait. Are you saying either a nymph or fairy could be responsible for killing the Ashton woman?"

"Yes." Why was he slow to recognize the significance of this news?

"Not possible. Fairies are sweet, and any kind of nymph, water or wood, is very mild-mannered. They wouldn't hurt any living creature."

Nikki sat down and picked Milo up. "That's a general statement that could also apply to witches, but we all know pricker bushes are hiding the garden."

"Did you overhear any tidbits from the argument?"

He directed his attention to me. "Finally, you're asking intelligent questions."

"You could just volunteer the information."

"How would that help you in your new position as head of the coven? You'll need to ask questions during meetings. I won't be there to assist. It's not a familiar's place. Of course, we're free to discuss various topics outside the meeting, and you have your book as long as you continue to read it."

"Milo, we can't worry about the future until we can solve the murder of Shula Ashton. Since magic is involved on so many levels, the police will have a harder time deciphering the clues."

"You're right. I'm sorry." He hopped onto the table and bobbed his head toward the chair beside Nikki. "Please, take a seat."

All I wanted to do was get on the road to Pine Valley and return in time to meet the team and Gage for lunch. Hopefully, we'll have news to share. I did as he asked.

Milo's ears flattened out to the sides like they did when he was pleased with himself or content. This time, I was leaning toward pleased.

"Now, back to your interest in the additional visitors for our visitors." He almost chuckled before coughing up a hairball. "Anyway, the women showed up around eleven. I know that because I was lying on the back of the new sofa in the front window getting some rays. By noon, the sun has moved overhead and I need to go outside to take another sun-snooze."

I went to the clue board. Drawing a line across the bottom, I jotted down *eleven* to the left of the line, two next to *text to Ambrose,* and *three-fifteen* when I discovered Shula. I didn't add the part where Milo contacted me. There was no way to explain that to a non-magical. He nodded his approval. "Then what happened?"

"At first, I didn't realize it was anything. They spread out a blanket and had a picnic. Not a spot I would have chosen, but who knows how far they'd been traveling, and it takes all kinds of people to find different places for lunch. They had just finished eating when a car rolled to a stop. Three people got out. Two women, which would have been the nymphs, and one man, which I'm pretty sure was a fairy, although he could have been a witch, hanging with the nymphs. I'd lean to the fairy."

"Do you know what time that was and what they looked like?" I would add these details while he talked.

"Twelve-thirty-ish. The male was tall, thin, and muscular but lean. He walked like his feet barely grazed the ground. The women were beautiful, with long flowing hair; they were tall and thin, too. They seemed shy until the argument started."

I put a note on the timeline for when the three newcomers arrived.

"Why do you say they seemed shy?" Nikki asked.

"They kept their heads down like a shy child does when speaking with people they don't know well."

I jotted that down. "Was anyone called by name?"

Milo looked at the ceiling. "Alder was the man. The women were Fern and Ivy, but don't ask me who was who. I only heard that much since I skulked over there."

I cocked a brow. "That was a risk. They might have realized you were my familiar."

"Nah, I circled around them. It wasn't like I strolled across the street from our front yard."

I exhaled, relieved. Milo was known to take chances, but I wished he wouldn't. "Did you hear what the argument was about?"

"No. It went on for maybe close to an hour.

It was four against three. If I had known something bad would happen, I would have hung around longer."

I looked at the timeline I created. "There are sixty minutes or so from when the fairy and nymphs showed up and when Ravena, Morgaine, and Violet left Shula. What did they do in that time?"

"Mostly bicker. At one time or another, they were all waving their arms around, jabbing fingers to make their points. You know, being mad. I'm sorry there isn't more to tell you."

"That's okay, Milo. Can you think of anything else that might be important?"

"Not a thing, but hey, cast a spell to make finding Ivy, Fern, and Alder easier when you get to Pine Valley. That would save you time."

Nikki grinned. "He's got a point."

Milo sat up straighter. "See, there's my contribution to the investigation. You're welcome."

I gave him a quick kiss on the head. "Smoked salmon tonight if you promise to watch the crime scene while we're gone. And if anything happens, you'll get in touch with me right away."

"A bubbling cauldron of happiness for you, my dear witch."

I peered out the windshield and tried to wrap my thoughts around all that had happened in less than twenty-four hours. "Nik, here's what I don't get. Aunt Mimi is a kind and reasonable witch. If the witches in Pine Valley wanted to join our coven again, why hadn't they approached the council before now? And don't say they were waiting for me; I don't buy it. Something's wonky."

She half turned in her seat, and looked at me. "I've been thinking about that and agree with you. They could have, even as witches our age, approached the coven. It's not like a bunch of old, cranky crones are sitting on the council. There's very little they say no to."

"What's the worst that could have happened?"

She shook her head. "They say no."

I held up my hand. "Wait. I don't think the council would have said no immediately. They'd ask for conditions to be met and a probationary period."

"No. That's what *you* would have done." She beamed. "You're going to make a great head of the coven."

I felt heat flush my cheeks. "Thanks, but Aunt Mimi would have done something similar."

"Maybe. Maybe not. I wasn't overly impressed with Violet, Ravena, and Morgaine when Gage interviewed them. They didn't seem that broken up over their friend's death. On the other hand, Ambrose's grief was palpable through the one-way mirror."

"That doesn't make them murderers. I'm leaning more toward the unexpected visitors. But why didn't the witches say anything about them?" I tapped my phone in the holder on the dash and then the speed dial button for Gage.

"Good morning, almost wife."

A smile blossomed on my face. "Good morning, almost husband."

Nikki looked out the window. I guessed it was her version of giving us privacy.

"Are you alone?"

He chuckled. "Yes. You've learned something interesting?"

"I talked with Milo this morning and discovered the witches weren't the only visitors from Pine Valley. There were two nymphs and one fairy that argued with them."

"Really?" I could picture him stroking his chin while he digested that information. "Any idea what time of day it was?"

"Milo said the witches arrived around eleven, and the newcomers showed up about an hour and a half later. The argument might have lasted another hour, and then they left."

"Since you don't mention the specifics about the argument, can I assume he didn't overhear it?"

"Not a word. But it was three against four. He said they left and didn't pay it any more attention since he assumed they left town. But Gage, what if they didn't?"

Nikki said, "Remember, the fairies and nymphs have a kind-hearted disposition. For one of them to have killed Shula is a stretch. My wand is on one of the three who didn't disclose all that happened yesterday."

"It does cause a new wrinkle. Why wouldn't they have wanted to transfer the suspicion to the others?"

"Gage, what if they didn't want me to know about the argument since it could color how I felt about them wanting to rejoin the coven?"

"That's a possibility. Are you on your way to Pine Valley now?"

"Yes, when we're off the phone, I'm going to do a locating spell for the nymphs and the fairy and get some answers before we leave town."

"All right. Call me when you're back in the car and keep your wand close, and please be careful."

"Wand: check—and I'm always careful." I touched my fingers to my lips, kissed them, and blew it to the phone. "I sent you a kiss for luck."

He chuckled. "Nikki, be careful."

"You can count on us."

I tapped the red button and disconnected the call before pulling to the side of the road, next to a large white sign that said, "Welcome to Pine Valley."

I closed my eyes, and Nikki took my hand. "Power boost."

I took three deep breaths. "Two nymphs and a fairy are sought. Guide Nikki and me to them without a thought. For they may hold the key to a mystery for which the guilty must concede. To pay for the crime indeed. For this I wish, so it shall be."

A ripple of pain rushed through me, and I dropped Nikki's hand before it would transfer to her. I wasn't fast enough.

Her face was ashen. "Did you feel that?"

I placed my hand on the center of my chest. "Don't ask me how I know, but the three are in danger. We have to hurry." I dropped the car into first gear, and my tires kicked up gravel as I peeled away from the side of the road.

Her eyes were wide with fear. "We're going to be too late for one."

I gripped the steering wheel tighter. I was unsure where to drive, but I trusted my magic would take us there. "I know."

We pulled into the driveway of a charming white cottage with pink shutters. The front door was standing open. I threw the car in park and turned the key while pushing open the door. My wand was in my hand, prepared to defend us. As I grew closer, I could see a body draped over the threshold. I held out my hand to slow us down. I stopped and strained to hear the mournful groan of the wind in the trees, almost as if they were sobbing.

"Who's there?" A voice echoed from some-where inside.

I glanced at Nikki, and she nodded. I was going in first. I knelt beside the body of a woman and touched her neck. There was no pulse.

"Lily Michaels and Nikki Twing. From Pembroke Cove." Adding that detail might show whoever was inside that I wasn't a random person.

"Prove it." The voice was bolder now.

Nikki shrugged and whispered, "Parlor tricks?"

"Lily Michaels, council leader of the Pembroke Cove Coven."

Chapter 12
Gage

I glanced at my phone as Lily's unique ringtone went off. "Lily? Are you okay?"

"We're fine, but I need the police and you, Sharon, Mac, and EL, to get to Pine Valley immediately. I texted you the address."

My stomach clenched, and a lump rose in my throat. "Why?"

"We're at Ivy and Fern's cottage. Ivy's dead. They're the nymphs who argued with the witches yesterday."

"Is it...?"

"Murder."

I slammed my fist against the desktop. "What in the stars is happening?"

"I'm not sure. If you're alone on the drive, call me. I'll fill you in on what we know. For now, I'll cast a protection spell to secure the crime scene. But Gage, hurry. This poor woman didn't even know it was coming. She was attacked from behind. Fern said she was on the opposite side of the house and didn't hear anything."

"Make sure you and Nikki are in a protection spell, too. I'll get there as fast as I can."

"Thanks. I don't know if the local police are witches so I won't mention magic."

"Good idea." I was already halfway down the back hall of the station. "I'll call from the car." Stashing my cell phone in my jeans pocket, I entered the break room. Peabody and Mac were going over notes.

"Get your gear and pick up EL. We're going to Pine Valley. I'll send you the address.

Lily and Nikki just found a dead body that I'm sure is connected to our case."

"How?" Sharon was putting a lid on her coffee and texting.

I assumed it was to EL. "Yesterday, when I interviewed the women, they never mentioned three people from Pine Valley argued with them outside Lily's house. Now one of them is dead."

Mac asked, "Lily found the body?"

"Yeah, she was going over to poke around and ask a few questions. You know, her normal gig, and her first stops were the three new suspects." Peabody and Mac followed me down the hall and out the door to the parking area. "Not questioning them like we would, more like, did you know Shula Ashton and the others in a friendly manner?"

He nodded. "Sounds like Lily's usual line of innocuous questions."

"As soon as they arrived at the cottage, they discovered one of the women, Ivy, no last name yet, had been murdered."

Peabody said, "Did they call the local police?"

"No, she asked me to." Dang it. I pulled out my phone and dialed.

A clipped greeting, "Chief Greenleaf," had me take a deep breath.

"Laurel. Gage Erikson."

"Well, Gage, I didn't expect to speak to you until your wedding. What's the occasion?"

"Unfortunately, I'm headed to Pine Valley with two detectives and Dr. Dawson. My fiancé, Lily, went to talk with a woman named Ivy and discovered her dead at her home. It could be connected to a case we're working so she called me."

"Ivy Fields? Dead? Who's at the scene with her?" The chief's tone had gone from friendly to all business.

"Nikki Twing and a woman, Fern. Other than that, they're alone and standing by to make sure no one disturbs the scene."

"I'm on my way." She disconnected.

"Did she tell you to stay away?" Mac asked

as Sharon got behind the wheel of their police-issued sedan.

"No. I'm sure she'll accept the help. Her team is small, and I mentioned we were bringing EL."

"That's good. We'll meet you there. Or do you want me to ride with you to discuss the case?"

"No. I will check in with Lily to stay on top of things." I opened the driver's door and gave him a curt nod. "See you there."

I waited for Sharon to leave the lot first. She turned in the direction of the hospital where EL would be.

I took the main road leading west to Pine Valley. I touched the necklace that Lily had given me. It was similar to the amulet she wore, and now it was cool under my fingertips. I wished there was a way to make sure she was safe, but the best I could do was get there as fast as possible. Not that Lily couldn't handle herself, but I didn't want her to be in any danger.

Now that I was on the road, I called her.

"Gage." Her voice was calm.

"I've marshaled the troops, and everyone is on their way. How are things there?"

"Steady. We have Fern outside with us. She's a mess and has no idea what happened. She and Ivy were having coffee when they heard a knock on the front door. Ivy went to answer it but when she didn't return to the kitchen, Fern thought she heard something, went to see what was taking her so long, and found her lying in the doorway. Then, we arrived."

"She didn't hear a car or anyone talking?" That was the first hole in this case. "Lily, you didn't say how she was killed other than she was attacked from behind."

"Well, you know how Shula Ashton was stabbed?"

I wouldn't say I liked where this was going, but I wished she would say *with a knife*. I took a half breath. "Let me guess, this same type of weapon was used on this woman?"

"I can only see part of it, but it looks to be the same approximate size, a dark-colored wood."

My grip on the steering wheel tightened. "You didn't touch anything, did you?" I hated the accusatory tone in my voice. "Sorry, force of habit."

"It's okay. I'm getting used to it. For the record, it's still annoying."

I could hear the attempt at lightness in her voice. "Noted." I tipped my head. "Do I hear a siren?"

"Yes. That must be the local officers."

"It'll be the chief. Her name is Greenleaf."

"Are you seeing a pattern here with the names?"

I could almost picture Lily with her right eyebrow arched over her deep brown eye. Her puzzle-loving mind had kicked into overdrive. "No. What am I missing?"

"So far, everyone we've encountered in connection with this case has a name that is somehow connected to nature, even the police chief."

"I'm not following you."

Lily's sigh was laced with frustration. "Ashton, Erickson, Rockford, Fields, Marshall, Perry, and now, Greenleaf. It either has the word spelled or its meaning is connected to the elements. I wish I'd put that together sooner."

I wasn't sure who all the other people were, but she'd explain soon. "Don't be so hard on yourself. I never connected the dots." Not that I would have. I'm not as well-versed in the meaning of names as Lily. She's in tune with the world around her while I focus on my job, family, and friends.

"Gage, I gotta go. The police chief just pulled up."

Before I could remind her of anything, she disconnected. I knew she could handle any situation, but I wondered about Laurel Greenleaf. Both her first and last names were related to plants. Could she be an elemental witch or maybe a descendant of one?

I still had fifteen minutes before I arrived at the scene, so I grabbed my cell phone and called the person I knew was an expert in local history.

"Dad, it's Gage."

"Hi, son. Are you calling for me to help you warm up your feet?"

"Huh? Oh, no. It's not about the wedding. I'm working on a case and on my way to Pine Valley. I want to pick your brain regarding the area's history."

"Happy to lend some brain power."

"Great. A woman I interviewed yesterday claimed we were cousins. She's from Pine Valley."

"Your mom said Lily asked her if there was a connection, and she also mentioned that Ravena Erikson is an air witch. Even with the same last name, we're not related. Has something else happened?"

I glanced at the phone and decided to be direct. "Do you know about the split between elemental witches and Pembroke Cove witches decades ago? With the elemental witches moving to Pine Valley?"

"I do. As I recall, several prominent families moved away. It was hard for them at first, with the well-established magical community, but eventually, they learned to co-exist peacefully. Why?"

"I'm curious if Pine Valley is one hundred percent magical?"

"The research shows most people living there are. However, some are like Lily's mom. They're intuitive but not fully developed as a witch. Why the questions?"

"A woman was killed in front of Lily's house yesterday, and today, another woman the victim was seen arguing with died. The first is reportedly an elemental witch and today's victim, a nymph."

He gave a low whistle. "That's not good. Any solid suspects?"

I shrugged my shoulders. It was not that Dad could see me, but maybe it'd release some of the tension I felt. "Until this morning, I would have said yes. Lily's at the scene, and she said it looks to be the same type of murder weapon."

"What's that?" Dad's tone grew more serious.

"EL thinks yesterday's weapon was a shard of yew wood honed into a dagger. Lily says this one today looks very similar." I wasn't sure who commented on the wood but I'd stick with EL for now.

He sucked in a breath. "I seem to recall reading something about a case like this years ago. If it would help, I can scan my books on Pine Valley's history and see what I can find."

The band that had been constricting my chest lessened a bit. This could be a solid lead. "Do you have time?"

"Sure. Your mom is off with Mindy doing some final shopping for the wedding."

I heard a snap of his fingers. "I just happened to think of something. Did you know that Mindy's maiden name was Waterson?"

"No." That was another branch connected

to one of my suspects. "Can you check something else for me?"

"Name it. I've never been this close to one of your investigations before, and it's exciting."

Dad loved a project. "Do you have access to genealogy information? Can you see how Mindy might be related to Morgaine Waterson? She was another of the elemental witches waiting outside Lily's yesterday. She's friends with our first victim and knew the second."

"I'll get right on that. Do you want me to call or text you what I find?"

"You can text any quick updates, and I'll swing by the house after lunch and you can fill me in." I hoped that would give him enough time.

"How much longer will you be in the car?"

I glanced at the clock on my dashboard. "Less than ten minutes."

"All right, I'll see what I can find out and be in touch. And Gage? Be extra careful. Whatever's going on with the residents of Pine Valley, someone's pretty ticked off."

After I disconnected, I let the facts swirl around in my brain. Why were some people connected but not witches like Mindy Michaels? Was it the luck of the draw that as people married non-magicals, potentially, their powers were diluted to the point they didn't exist, and was that part of the issue with the folks in Pine Valley? Jealousy? That was an excellent motive for murder, and it wasn't that much of a stretch if the second was to keep someone quiet.

What if Shula and her friends wanted to approach Lily about joining the coven, but the newcomers tried to stop them? Could they have felt rejoining wasn't in the best interest of the witch, nymph, and fairy communities? That would be a powerful motive. But which one would have killed both? I knew I was jumping to a conclusion before the facts were in, but what if the same type of weapon had killed a witch and a nymph and maybe even came from the same tree? Laughing at myself, I realized I wasn't a detective who leaped to conclusions but relied on facts.

Maybe Lily's way of investigating was rubbing off on me. She'd laugh if I told her that. She was a puzzle master, and I doggedly followed each clue in a linear pattern.

At the moment this case didn't make sense. I couldn't remember the last time two victims within twenty-four hours were linked to the same crime.

When the phone rang, I didn't take my eyes off the road as I navigated the sharp corner. "Detective Erikson."

"Son. I have some information for you. Mindy is a fourth cousin to Morgaine Waterson, the current and only member of her immediate family to live in Pine Valley. She has a sister and a brother, but they've relocated to other parts of the country. I'll put the specifics in an email."

"That would explain why Mindy is sensitive but not a full witch like Lily. She comes from an elemental line."

"Right. Inheriting magic is like inheriting eye or hair color. The gene could pop up or dilute over time, and Morgaine Waterson is a powerful water witch. I dug into some newspaper archives and her temper is reported to have caused large and dangerous water spouts of bodies of water, rivers, lakes, or the ocean."

"Good to know. Anything else?"

"Unfortunately, no, but I'll keep digging. You can read my report when you're free."

"Thanks, Dad. I appreciate your support. Please keep this under wraps for now. I don't want Mom or Mindy to worry about what's happening."

"I don't keep secrets from your mother." His tone was stern, and I knew they had a relationship based on honesty.

"I'm not asking you to lie to her. This is an ongoing investigation, and I can't have information leaked to the public until we're ready to make a statement." I wasn't asking him to be dishonest; I needed time to do my job, and I wanted him to respect my position.

"That I can do. We'll talk soon."

"Bye, Dad." I slowed the car and peered through the windshield. Lily's blue and white Mini Cooper was parked beside a black hybrid vehicle. I pulled behind them, blocking their exit, and next to the black and white SUV. Before I could get out, Peabody pulled in behind me. Three doors opened on the sedan and EL, carrying his backpack, and Mac, his evidence case, strode between them, stopping in front of my car.

I shut my door and gave them a curt nod. "Are we ready to do this?"

EL bobbed his head in the direction of the chief. "Any information about this crime?"

I nodded. "I spoke to Lily, and she isn't certain, but she thinks it's the same type of weapon used on Shula Ashton and, like before, the attack came from behind. Our victim had to have known the killer to have felt comfortable turning their back on them."

"What other details do you have?" Peabody rested her hands on her belt.

"Per Fern, who was here at the time, Ivy Fields went to answer the door, but she never cried out. Fern heard a soft thud and came to the front of the house to investigate."

"Gage?" Lily was running in our direction. "Come quick."

Chapter 13
Lily

My breath stuttered in my lungs. Chief Greenleaf pointed to a jagged-edged piece of paper under poor Ivy's body.

"Has anyone touched this?"

I shook my head. "Nikki took Fern out back to wait, and I stayed here to keep an eye on things."

She gave me a sharp look. "I've heard how you've helped Detective Erikson and the Pembroke Cove Police Department solve other murders, but other than giving your statement, I won't require your amateur assistance."

The sneer on her face spoke volumes—she didn't think much of me. All she wanted me to do was tell her what I knew or saw and then disappear.

I leaned closer to see if there were words written on the paper.

The chief put her body between me and the new evidence. Why hadn't I seen that earlier?

Resting her hand on her weapon, she demanded, "Tell me what you know."

I couldn't see her eyes due to her mirrored aviator-style sunglasses. "Where do I start?"

"Why are you in Pine Valley?"

The hair on the back of my neck stood at attention. Her curt tone made me feel more like a suspect and less like a helpful bystander. The crunch of tires in the driveway drew my attention, and relief washed over me. "Be right back."

"Gage?" I ran in his direction. "Come quick."

He moved toward me. "What's wrong?"

"Chief Greenleaf is acting like I'm guilty of a crime, maybe even this one. And," I glanced over my shoulder as I felt the weight of her stare. "She wants to know why I'm in Pine Valley. I can't tell her I'm trying to figure out why these people wanted to talk to me and had gone so far as to wait outside my house." My stomach flipped as unease settled.

I gave Sharon, Mac, and EL a grateful smile. It was good to see their familiar faces.

Sharon gave a decisive nod. "Lily, it will be fine once we tell her you're an unpaid asset to the force."

"I'm glad one of us thinks so." I took Gage's hand. "I hate to ask, but can you stay with me while she questions me?"

"Absolutely." He gestured in Greenleaf's direction. "The sooner she stops focusing on an innocent person, the quicker we can find the guilty one."

"Boss," Mac said, "We're going to examine the body and document the scene."

Gage didn't acknowledge Mac. But they were a well-oiled machine. It wasn't necessary; everyone had a job and was more than capable of carrying it out.

As we drew closer to the chief, her facial expression never wavered. There was none. She gave a curt nod. "Detective. You made good time."

"Yes." He nodded in the direction of his team. "Any concerns with them getting to work?"

"None at all. Glad for the help." Her mouth dipped into a frown. "I was getting ready to question Ms. Michaels."

At least she knew my name. Gage must have told her, but that didn't matter. "Do you mind if Gage is here?"

"No, it'll help speed up this process and get you on the road."

I wanted to say, *HA*, like I was going anywhere, but I didn't.

"Let's start with why you picked today to come to Pine Valley and stop at Fern's house and, on top of that, stumble over her body?" She crossed her arms over her mid-section, and her mirrored gaze never wavered.

"Yesterday, a woman was killed across the street from my home. When the suspects were interviewed, we were told they had been waiting to speak with me."

"About what?"

I heard the suspicion in her voice. "I'm not sure." I crossed my fingers behind my back. "This morning, I learned Fern Marshall and Ivy Fields argued with the deceased, Shula Ashton, also outside my home."

"Who provided you with this information? And why wasn't Fern or Ivy questioned yesterday? Oh, right, you conveniently found out this morning."

Her snide tone was becoming intolerable and I had enough. "Chief Greenleaf, why are you talking to me like I'm a suspect in this case?

Detectives Erikson, Peabody, Sullivan, or Dr. Barrett can vouch for my character."

She lifted her chin. "Everyone is a suspect until I can prove otherwise."

Gage narrowed his gaze. "Chief, my detectives came to assist in your investigation. I would ask that you rethink your decision to treat Ms. Michaels as a suspect."

She dropped her arms and took one menacing step in my direction. "Fine. I don't like you, so watch your step."

"You don't even know me." I stepped forward. Gage grabbed my arm, applying slight pressure to slow me down.

"But I *do*." She stalked toward EL, who was examining the victim.

"Gage, I've done nothing to that woman. I've never even met her. Why is she being so hateful?"

He pulled me away from everyone and lowered his voice. "I think it has to do with you assuming the role in the coven. I was talking to Dad on the way over. All the names of people in town are tied back to the elements. It makes sense. Even your mom's maiden name is Waterson. I know she's not a witch, but what if her magic was diluted over generations? Like Erikson might have been."

"Does that have any bearing on what's happening now?"

He shook his head. "I don't think so. I just found it interesting. But I think both murders are tied to your coven. I'm just not sure if they wanted to be included or if some of the group wanted to be excluded."

"That doesn't change that two women are dead and more than likely by the same hand." I chewed my bottom lip. "There's a note under the body. I need to know what's written on it."

"Lily, I can't share information on this case like I have in the past. This is technically out of my jurisdiction."

"Then why did you bring EL, Sharon, and Mac?" I blew out my breath in a huff, ruffling my bangs. "Because they're familiar with Shula's case?"

He gave me a tentative smile. "This is frustrating. I get that. Let me see what I can learn. Wait with Nikki and Fern. I'll come find you when I can."

I shook my head. "Not a chance. I want to witness whatever's going to happen firsthand."

Gage gave me a wink. "I should get back. Care to wander a little closer?"

He didn't have to suggest that twice. My fingertips tingled at the thought of being close to the actual investigation. I moved to the side of the yard but within line of sight. I could hear every detail shared between the detectives and the chief.

EL pointed to the shard of wood jutting from the victim's upper back and neck. As you can see," he said, holding up his phone, "this is strikingly similar to yesterday's victim. The wood is the same color, and my preliminary conclusion is they were made from the same piece of wood. I can confirm after I conduct testing."

"Estimated time of death?" Gage pointed to the paper and Sharon nodded.

"Roughly sixty minutes give or take." EL looked at me. "When did you arrive?"

I cleared my throat. "Forty-five minutes or so." A shiver raced down my spine as I realized I had come close to witnessing the attack. "Why do you think only one woman was attacked?"

Chief Greenleaf frowned. "The killer didn't realize there were two people in the house. If they had, it's logical: they would have searched for Fern and harmed her as well."

That didn't make sense. These had to be specific crimes. The only way to learn the truth was for Nikki and me to find Violet, Morgaine, and Ravena. They'd be able to shed light on the argument and, with some persuasion, tell me what the real story was behind wanting to talk with me.

Before we left, I wanted to catch a glimpse of that paper. Sharon moved around the area, taking many pictures from different angles. "EL, are you ready to move the body?"

"As soon as the EMTs arrive. Chief, I'm going to have the body taken to Pembroke Cove. It will be easier for me to compare evidence."

She jerked her head in agreement. "Fine. I want to be kept in the loop on all aspects of the crime. This was one of my people. I'll make sure whoever's responsible is brought to justice."

"Laurel, two murders and most likely one killer." Gage's voice was steady, but I was confident his logic annoyed her; in some small way, he claimed dibs on the case.

An uneasy silence cloaked the scene. But was it one murderer? With so many people involved, it could be a duo.

"Where does Alder Perry live?"

The chief slowly turned. "Stay away from him."

"May I speak with you a moment?" I gestured to the parked police vehicles. I was done with her attitude. If I couldn't figure out what I might have done to tick her off, I'd leave, but I was going to try.

"Detective. I'll be right back."

Gage gave me an encouraging wink after she turned her back to him. "Take your time."

I led the way, and when I felt comfortable that we could speak freely, I stopped. "Chief Greenleaf. We've gotten off on the wrong foot, and I'm not sure why."

She snorted. "Four women went to have a simple conversation with you, and three came home. Now, another woman who also went to Pembroke Cove has been killed. Are you seeing a pattern here? I don't want you talking to anyone in my town. Go home, Lily, and let the professionals do their jobs."

"Chief, I had nothing to do with anyone's death. I wasn't home when the women came and camped across from my house. Maybe they should have called first. Since I couldn't have that conversation with any of them, I'm in the dark about the true nature of their visit. Would you care to enlighten me since you seem to be in the know?"

"I know who you are." She jabbed her finger in the direction of my chest but didn't touch me. "Lily Michaels. Mimi's niece. You think you're something special. I know that until a few years ago, you knew nothing about everything I hold dear. Now you've become so great," she waved her hands like she was performing a jazz dance, "that it's given people ideas that change is coming. You're nothing special."

I placed my hand over my amulet. It was cool to the touch. Even if I wasn't in danger, my temper spiked. How long could I keep my cool was the big question. In all my life, I'd never been so rudely spoken to.

"I don't know what you consider special. But I'm a good person *and* a good witch." My words came out like a hiss. I didn't care if she was a non-magical. At that moment, she knew who and what I was, and I didn't appreciate being painted as a villain in this or any instance.

"I'm getting married in a few days. Imagine my surprise when I learned, less than twenty-four hours ago, that my life would change again. It's an honor to replace my aunt on the council. If anyone wants to discuss any issue with me, I'll listen with an open mind. But if everyone in Pine Valley is like you, it will make my job harder; but I've got the chops to handle the job. I will do what's best for everyone and not just to suit a select few."

Her brow cocked and a small smile played over her face. "Are you saying you'll welcome anyone from Pine Valley into your circle?"

I threw up my hands, exasperated. "What I'm saying is I'll be fair."

"Do you even understand the ramifications of agreeing to unify the two groups?"

I drummed my fingers against my leg to dissipate some of my frustration with this annoying person. "No. I haven't been told what the Pine Valley people want to accomplish by coming together. Do you know what they wanted to talk about?"

"I do. It's not my place to say. Shula was our council spokesperson, and now someone else must step up." She pushed back the brim of her cap and took off her sunglasses, massaging the bridge of her nose. "Look. I've got nothing against you personally. I don't know you, and Gage—I respect the man. If you're good enough for him to marry you, you gotta be decent."

"I hear a but in your words."

"Yeah, but, in regards to this situation, and not the murders, which is just awful, but the other, I'm taking the wait-and-see approach. If you don't screw up, then we might get along."

I narrowed my eyes and tipped my head. "Your interpretation of my not doing something correctly is subjective."

She smirked. "True. I like that you're quick on your feet and have a sharp mind. Maybe there is something about this case that you'll figure out, and it'll help bring the killers to justice."

"Killer. Same method. The same weapon isn't a coincidence. It was only a matter of time until someone came forward about yesterday's argument. Even if Violet, Ravena, or Morgaine didn't tell the police. Which could have prevented this death had we known."

"You have a point." She glanced over her shoulder. "With solid police work, maybe we can ensure this spree is over."

"If you mean that, let me do what I do best. Dissect clues and unravel the puzzle." I stuck my hand out, unsure if she'd accept my attempt at an olive branch.

She looked at it before meeting my eyes. With a firm grip on my hand, she stared me down. "Lily, don't make me regret this."

I held her hand as tight as she did mine. "You won't." Finally, we had come to an understanding, and I could get back to what I loved to do; solve a puzzle, even if it was murder. I dropped her hand and nodded in the direction of the crime scene. "After you."

Chapter 14
Lily

As I approached Gage, he was kneeling next to the body. His eyes widened briefly as Chief Greenleaf announced I was to be included in the investigation update.

EL winked at me, and Sharon turned away, her lips tipped into a smile. I kept my face neutral, wanting to pay close attention to what was being said and not give the chief any reason to change her mind.

Gage stood. "Chief, as Dr. Barrett mentioned, this is similar to the attack on Ms. Ashton. The only difference we can note is the slip of paper." He nodded in the direction of the ambulance. "In a moment, we should have access to that without risk of damaging it."

She glanced at her watch and looked toward the street. "I wonder where my officer is?"

I certainly didn't have an answer to that question. I pointed to the backyard. "I'm going to check on Nikki and Fern."

Gage nodded, and I slipped away. I didn't want to witness the EMTs moving Ivy's body, even if I might get a look at the paper. With this new understanding between the chief and me, I didn't have to sneak looks.

I came around the side of the house. Nikki and Fern were facing each other at a small bistro table. Nikki held Fern's hand and spoke in a comforting tone, "There was nothing you could have done."

Fern cried softly. "If I had gone with her, I could have prevented this from happening, or at least I would have seen who was at the door."

I pulled out a chair and sat next to Fern.

Taking her other hand, I glanced at Nikki, who lifted a shoulder, indicating she was happy to let me take the lead.

"Fern, look at me."

She lifted her tear-stained face.

"There is no way to know if you could have prevented what happened. If whoever did this was intent on harming Ivy, they would have. Maybe not this morning, but at some point soon."

"But," her words came out in a stutter, "she died alone."

I maintained steady eye contact with her. "Sadly, she did. Do you think she would have wanted you to put yourself in harm's way?"

She shrugged her shoulders.

"There *is* something you can do."

"What?" She hiccupped softly.

"Tell me everything about this morning that you can remember." I also wanted to drill her on yesterday's events, but one step at a time.

"Today was my turn to make coffee. We've been roommates since we graduated. She inherited her grammy's house and didn't charge me to live here. Mostly, we split the bills and shared food. She's my best friend." Fresh tears slipped down her face. "She was."

I pulled my chair closer and wrapped my arm around her shoulders. "Ivy sounds terrific."

In a wail, she cried, "Why would someone want to hurt her?"

I hugged her a little tighter. "Back to coffee. You both were in the kitchen?"

She sniffed. "Yes. We wanted to sit out here and talk about," she paused, "things before we went to work. She had just come in the house from drying off the chairs."

"And there was a knock on the front door?" Nikki gently tried to steer her back to the critical thread.

"Yeah." She closed her eyes. "Two knocks, a pause, and two more. Almost like whoever it was didn't think we heard the first two."

I maintained my focus on her. "Then what happened? Did you hear Ivy talking to someone? Please close your eyes and think about it. Put yourself back in the kitchen."

"Can we go inside? Maybe if I'm standing in the exact spot I was in when she went to answer the door, it will help."

Nikki pushed back her chair. "Should I check with Gage?"

"Please."

"Tell me what happened yesterday at my house. I know you, Ivy, and Alder had an argument with Shula and the others."

She pulled back and put as much distance as possible between us, based on how close we were sitting. "How do you know about that?"

"There's a witness who came forward this morning. He said you arrived around twelve-thirty, argued, and left about an hour later."

"Same old argument, just a different place and day."

"I don't understand what you mean. But I'd like to."

She patted her pocket. "I need a tissue."

I said a quick spell and withdrew a travel pack from my bag. "Here you go."

"Thanks." She blew her nose and balled up the tissue in her hand. "We were fighting about the council, your council."

At least I knew she knew I was a witch. "What specifically?" I wasn't about to make any snap judgments on what it might have been about.

She sighed. "I guess you'll find out sooner or later. We, the fairies and nymphs, want to talk to you and the council about becoming a part of the community again. Shula and other elemental witches don't."

"Why not?" Considering this was the opposite of what I had been told yesterday, I needed to figure out who was telling the truth.

"Back in the day, you know, we were one coven, the PV contingent and Pembroke Cove,"

"PV as in Pine Valley?"

She nodded. "Yes. It's easier to call them or us, PV. Like I said, the elemental witches lumped our kind in with them, and we all got cast out. The fairies and nymphs were innocent bystanders in the fallout. We were happy just to be happy and do our own thing." A dark cloud slipped over her face as her brows knitted together and her lips thinned. "Shula was going to ruin our chance of being reunited. We wanted to approach your council as two separate groups, but they said it was all of us from PV or no one."

"That must have made you mad."

Her head bobbed. "Alder and I couldn't believe Shula's audacity."

"Did Ivy feel the same way?"

"We all did." She stood as Nikki approached the table.

"The chief said as long as we stay in the kitchen, we can go inside."

My chair legs caught on the grass as I got up from the chair. "Are you sure going inside won't be hard on you?"

"I have to do all I can to help bring this horrible person to justice." She straightened her shoulders, snapped her head in a curt nod, and marched in front of me and Nikki to the back door.

She hesitated on the threshold, raised her fist to her lips, and bowed her head. We waited a few steps behind her, giving her a moment to gather her thoughts.

I had never been in her exact shoes before. I felt pain rolling off her, like angry waves crashing against the shore at the height of a hurricane. Placing my hand on her shoulder, I closed my eyes, sending her comfort, and let it drop to my side.

She took several deep breaths and thrust her shoulders forward and back. "I'm ready," she said and stepped inside. She crossed to the counter where the coffee pot sat and pushed the button to turn the pot off. "Do you want me to reenact what I was doing?"

"Just a second." I hurried over to the arch where the hallway began. The front door was open, and Sharon was with EL. I asked, "When I go back inside, can you say how long it will take to confirm the wood? I need to know if

Fern could have overheard any potential argument at the front door."

EL gave a brisk nod. "You got it."

I returned to the kitchen. "Okay, where were you standing when you heard the first two knocks on the door?" I gestured for Nikki to stand in the hallway, and I stood next to Fern.

She pointed to a cabinet above the coffee maker. "I got the filter and coffee from here and had just finished scooping coffee. When we heard the first two knocks, Ivy handed me the pot of water. She said she'd get the door."

"Close your eyes and put yourself back in that moment."

She did as I asked and frowned. "Ivy pushed the kitchen chair in after she tripped over it. I heard her open the door and say hi." Her eyes were still closed.

"Can you hear someone answer her?"

Her lips morphed into a small smile. "Yes, it was a woman. But I'm not sure who it was as I didn't recognize her voice."

"You're sure it was female?" I tapped my

ear at Nikki, and she nodded. She could hear people talking near the door, but I heard faint murmurs.

"Pretty sure. But it wasn't a young voice, someone more mature—a deeper tone." She opened her eyes. "Does that mean anything to you?"

"Not yet, but please don't worry. We'll figure out who hurt Ivy."

Her chin wobbled as fresh tears appeared in her eyes. "I wish I could turn back the clock, and I had answered the door. She's been my best friend my entire life. What am I going to do without her?"

Nikki rushed forward and wrapped her arms around Fern. "She'll always be with you in your heart."

"I'll be back." I slipped out the back and jogged around the house as the ambulance doors closed. EL smacked them twice. The vehicle's lights came on as they turned down the driveway.

Sharon snapped photos of where Ivy had

fallen, including close-up shots of the paper. Mac opened an evidence bag and nodded to me. "Lily, do you want a picture of this?"

I withdrew my cell and didn't look at Gage or the chief. I rapidly tapped the photo button on my cell, noticing the word, *SPA*, before I stashed it.

"Gage, I was talking with Fern about what happened, and she thinks it was a woman at the door."

"She told you that? Does she say who specifically?"

"No." I tucked my hands into my pockets. "You should question her. Push on the fact that she said she could hear Ivy say hello."

Chief Greenleaf leaned in. "Do you have reason to doubt her?"

I tipped my head in the direction of the house. "Nikki could hear Sharon's conversation when she was standing at the hallway entrance, but I couldn't next to the coffee pot. All I could discern were voices. If Fern was where she said she was, she couldn't have heard Ivy say hello, much less that it was a woman."

"Do you think she was eavesdropping and heard the conversation?"

I widened my eyes. "Yes, and she might even know who it was specifically and doesn't want to say it out of fear. I don't think she should stay alone out here. It's pretty isolated."

"That's easy to manage. The scene needs to stay secured until I decide to release it. We'll find someplace for Fern to stay until then. Lily, is she in the kitchen?"

"Yes. Nikki's with her."

"I'll go talk to her." She strode around the house, and I pulled Gage aside when she was out of earshot. "I need to talk to you."

He said, "I hope you have some good information. We're coming up empty."

His back was to the team, and I faced him. This way, if Sharon or Mac approached, I could quickly divert the conversation so as not to spill the cauldron about witches among us.

"I casually asked her about what happened

yesterday. Fern said the argument with Shula revolved around them not wanting her to approach the council about the reconciliation of witches, but other members of the nymphs and fairies of Pine Valley did."

His brow furrowed. "That's the direct opposite of what Violet and the others said. They want to rejoin."

"I know. So, what if the killer wanted to silence Shula for her vocal opposition to the idea, and that same person thought Ivy shouldn't have interfered."

"That doesn't jibe. Shula was opposed, and Ivy wanted the merge. If that were the case, having two killers would have been logical." His lips twisted. "That wouldn't work, either. If the weapons are from the same source, it must be one person."

"Or one group. Violet, Ravena, and Morgaine all said they wanted to become a part of the Pembroke Cove coven, and if Shula was the holdout, maybe what we were told was partially the truth."

"With Shula out of the way, they could approach the council with the fairies and nymphs."

I slapped my hand against my leg. "Exactly. A unified group can be more persuasive."

"I need you and Nikki to find the other witches and talk to them. I still don't know how to explain to Sharon and Mac why anyone wanted to come to town and talk to the council. It's not like this is easy to explain to non-magicals."

"If we have to say something, we can say it's a charity that wants to remain anonymous." With a snap of my fingers, I grinned. "Like benevolent benefactors and keeping the members secret helps us do good work for the towns we serve."

"That could work. They know you got a lot of help when you had to step in and do the haunted house."

"Right. Even if that ended up with a few hiccups of its own." I nodded. "We're on to something, but we'll only use it if we have to."

Gage placed his hands on my arms. "Contact Mimi so she can speak with the council members this morning. We'll need their support because this will come out soon, and the sooner, the better, so we can solve these murders and refocus our attention on our special day."

I leaned in and kissed his lips. "Not the best way to start our marriage. Solving two murders, me taking over the council, and the stars only know what else."

"All that doesn't matter as long as we have each other." He wrapped his arms around me, holding me close. "Who knows, being the husband of the head witch could have perks."

I laughed. "Only you can take all the stress and try and spin it to a benefit."

"That's why you keep me around." He kissed my forehead. "Be safe when you talk to the women, and try to see Ambrose, too. He might know how his sister felt. Out of everyone, he could be the most honest, with his only driving force to find his sister's murderer."

I hugged him a little tighter before I let go. "You be careful, too."

He touched the middle of his shirt. "My warning system is as cool as a cucumber."

I tipped my head and looked into his eyes. "It's an amulet imbued with very special magic. Including protection and the most important attribute, love." I gave him a final quick kiss. "Now, to find my Watson so we can get our sleuth on."

Chapter 15
Gage

I popped the trunk on the car and called to Mac, "Ride with me."

He gave me a thumbs up as a response and continued methodically putting gear away. I needed to bounce ideas off someone and with Lily and Nikki chatting up potential suspects, I wasn't leaning in their direction. I needed to get my team back to the station and start doing the work, fingerprints, motives, and we needed to interview Fern Marshall.

Laurel strode in my direction. "Gage, wait up."

I met her halfway. "We're heading back."

"Good. I assume you want to talk with Fern and Alder Perry at the station. I could drive them both over."

I had so much going on—the murder, wedding, moving, and now this murder—that Alder Perry had fallen off my radar, but Laurel picked up the slack. "What time do you think you can bring them by?"

"I left a message for Alder. I'll text you as soon as he gets back to me." She nodded in the direction of the house. "Fern needs some time to pack a bag. I left a message with Ambrose, she might be able to stay with him for a few days."

I pushed my sunglasses to the bridge of my nose, more to take a beat and think. "Are you sure that's a good idea? They're all in the same boggy terrain."

"I know they're connected to both crimes,

so putting them together could add pressure for our attacker to strike again."

"We can't compromise their safety to flush out the killer."

She glanced over her shoulder and noticed Mac was packing up. "Do you think Lily could drop a protection charm? You know, to keep them safe?"

I nodded. "It's possible, but if one of the six is the killer and we haven't protected them all that'll make things worse."

She wrinkled her nose. "True, but I don't think Fern could have hurt Ivy. They've been so close and shared a home. And Ambrose harming his sister? Not a chance. He was fiercely protective of her. But it's possible he could have harmed Ivy. The women would have told him about the confrontation."

"Stranger things have happened. I've seen a lot, and most murders are committed by someone the victim knows."

"I know the statistics, Gage; you don't need to remind me. But you're right. Protecting two and not protecting them all isn't my best idea." She hooked her thumb on her belt. "Forget I suggested it."

"You got it." Mac walked in our direction. I dropped my voice. "No more talk of magic."

He acknowledged Laurel with a nod. "Chief."

"Detective, thanks for coming out today. It's good to have support and your expertise."

Mac glanced at me. "No thanks necessary. We've gotten too much practice in the last few years investigating murders." He stowed the case in the trunk and shut the lid. "Boss, Peabody's going to drop EL at the morgue so he can get started on the exam. She'll wait to see if she can lift prints from the weapon's handle and then head back to the station."

"That makes sense. Laurel, I'll let you know our progress. Text me as soon as you know when you're coming into the station with Alder Perry and Fern. I'll have a conference room ready."

She shook my hand. "Appreciate your help, Detective," and headed to the house.

I looked at the crime scene tape that wafted on the breeze. "Mac, come over here for a second and look."

He strode around the front of the car, and I moved away from it so he could have the same vantage point. "What do you see?"

"The outline of cones we placed around the body."

"Right, but look where the head was positioned."

"I'm not sure I see what you're getting at." His eyes squinted as he studied the scene.

"If Ivy had answered the door and then turned her back on the killer, she should have fallen inside at ninety degrees to the threshold. Instead, she crumpled to the ground. Her head was turned looking inside, and her body was on the step."

"Probably, she wanted to cry for help but couldn't." He pulled out his phone. "I'm going to have EL check for marks on her face as if someone clamped a hand over her mouth to prevent her from calling out to Fern."

"That's what I was thinking. Or did she look inside as she was dying, hoping the killer wouldn't go after Fern, too?"

Mac looked me in the eyes. "Or Fern is the killer. She had the opportunity, and there was no witness to say it wasn't her."

"We need to talk to Alder Perry and get his story about yesterday."

Mac nodded briskly. "I'll let Peabody know we're going to be conducting an interrogation, so if EL can confirm whether something was held over the victim's mouth, it could prove useful."

I took a final look at the peaceful setting before I got into the car—two homes in quiet settings and two murders. A chill raced down my spine. We'd find the guilty party before the end of the day.

.   .   .

Once back at the station, I got a coffee and checked my phone messages and texts—nothing from Lily, which was a good sign that she was doing her thing. However, I was curious if she had discovered anything that might help me.

There was a message from Mimi. *Can you come to the bookstore?*

I stashed my cell and looked for Mac, but he wasn't around. On my way through the lobby, I saw our receptionist at the front desk. "Hi, Alice. Will you let Mac know I ran over to the bookstore? I don't expect to be gone long."

"Of course."

Before she could ask questions, I was out the door and jogging down the steps. The Cozy Nook Bookstore wasn't far; it was quicker and easier to cross the town square than try and find a parking place. Besides, fresh air always cleared the spider webs from my brain.

The OPEN sign was on the door, and the tiny bell jingled when I entered. Nate was carrying a box of books to Mimi, standing by the new book table. Milo wasn't in his usual spot on the window seat.

"Gage. It's good of you to come by. I want to tidy the bookstore before Lily gets back. She's been working so hard, and with the wedding and now this new case, well, you know the Michaels witches, there are times when doing mundane tasks, the non-magical way, is best."

Mimi rambled just like Lily did, and it was sweet. "Where's Milo?"

"At home. Lily asked him to watch the crime scene, so he's taken up his spot in the front window, and Brutus was sleeping on the sofa when we left."

At least the four-legged family members were accounted for. "Milo would do anything for Lily."

"Now, wipe that worried wrinkle from your brow. Lily's just fine and dandy. Nikki's with her, and if she runs into any trouble, she knows how to get help. Besides, I added a little something extra to her and Nikki's protection spell before they left."

I strode across the room and wrapped my arms around Mimi. "Thank you for looking out for them."

She patted my back. "I always will. Even though she will soon be the top witch, she'll have me in her corner, fighting the good fight against the bad guys. Which is why I called you."

I took Nate's stack of books and set them on the table. "Did you discover something new?"

"Yes, but I knew not to touch it, so I added a protective bubble. One the non-magicals can't see, and only one of your detectives will be able to pick the item up."

I had to admire the quick thinking. "What was it and where?"

"Well, I was walking along the stand of trees, closer to Lily's house, and I noticed an area of decomposing leaves that seemed to have been disturbed recently. Don't worry. I was careful and used magic, so I've left no evidence of myself, but there's a handbag under there.

I'm confident you'll find it's Shula's once it's recovered."

"Hm. How am I going to explain where Mac should look?"

"I left the buckle partially exposed. You could tell him that I looked around, saw it, and told you."

"Did you find anything else?"

"No. But I can say that no one tried to get through the protection spell I put around the crime scene. Of course, your police officer, Jessie Shepard, and that nice young man, Jonesy, were able to patrol the area safely."

I kissed her on the cheek. "Thanks. This is great information. Make sure to come by the house for lunch. We're going to have a debrief."

"I wouldn't miss it. Besides, Nate and I are bringing the meal, so we have to be there."

Her words faded as I was already opening the door. I needed Mac to get to Lily's, retrieve the bag, and return to town as quickly as possible. I had a murder board to update. Lily's attention to detail was far superior to mine, and I had been doing this a lot longer. I couldn't help but grin. That's why we made a great pair.

Mac strode into my office and held up a clear evidence bag. "Right where Mimi said. Dang, she's got eagle eyes. I can't believe we missed this yesterday."

I was prepared for this comment. "An animal could have been digging around there looking for grubs overnight and exposed the buckle."

"True. Peabody's back, and she's setting up the conference room. I'll take this to evidence storage, check the contents, and hopefully, we'll discover a clue that will help."

"Excellent. Chief Greenleaf will be here with Fern Marshall and Alder Perry in thirty minutes. I'll ask Peabody to sit in with Fern, and I'd like you to sit in when I question Alder Perry."

"I'll be there." He turned and paused in the doorway. "Have you heard from Lily?"

I frowned. "Not yet, and I'm getting a little concerned. I thought she'd be back by now. It seems I'm in a holding pattern."

He looked at my clue board. "You've been busy."

There was so much I couldn't put on the board if the real motive were about the magicals from Pine Valley wanting to rejoin the Pembroke Cove coven.

"Do you remember that club Lily and Nikki are a part of?"

His brow furrowed. "Sorta. She doesn't talk about it much."

"For some reason, it might be tied to the four ladies coming to town."

"Really? That's odd. Did they want to join?"

Nodding, I chewed the inside of my cheek. "Possibly. I hope to know more when she gets back."

A quizzical look flashed over his face, but he didn't ask the question I knew he had. He held up the bag again. "I'm going to take care of this, and we can talk more after the interviews."

I sat in my chair. Silent. Reviewing the board yet again.

Victims: Shula Ashton, Ivy Fields—Stabbed, Yew Wood
Suspects: Violet Rockford, Ravena Erikson, Morgaine Waterson, Ambrose Ashton, Alder Perry, Fern Marshall
Motive: Join the group?
The argument between Shula, Ivy, with all except Ambrose.
Ambrose Ashton: Check alibi for Ivy
Fern Marshall?
Victims alone when attacked from behind
Ivy: paper, SPA

But where were the women when Shula was attacked? Had my team double-checked their alibis? I called Shepard since I could speak freely to him.

"Officer Shepard."

"Jessie, It's Detective Erikson."

"Hello, sir, how can I help?"

I didn't bother to make idle conversation. There would be time for that later. "Did you or Jonesy check out the alibi for the women?" I didn't want to use the word witch, just in case a non-magical walked by my office.

"Yes, sir. Jonesy and I are headed to the station with our report."

"Give me the highlights."

"The women did go to the beach like they claimed. Well, at least their car was in the parking lot, but once they locked it, they didn't appear on the cameras until much later."

I sat up in my chair. "How much later?"

"Forty-five minutes."

I pressed my fingers to my eyes. Lily's house was only twenty minutes away if you strolled. "Did you check around the marina to see if anyone saw them?"

"Jonesy and I canvased the area. No one claims to have seen them. At that time of day, everyone is either on boats or planning to take out new groups for fishing."

"Anything else?"

"No. Do you still want me to report to the station?"

"Yes, I'm going to interview two more suspects, and I want you to see if you can identify them from the beach security cameras."

"I'll be there in less than five minutes. Have you set up in conference room Alpha?"

I smiled. "Affirmative."

"Detective?" He paused, so I waited. "Do you want us to drive by Lily's before we head in?"

"She's not home. Milo and Brutus are standing watch."

I heard Jonesy snicker. "We'll run by just to make sure everything is okay. It'll only take an extra minute or two."

Jessie knew Milo could get in touch if necessary; however, there was no way to explain a talking cat to Jonesy. "That'd be great. Thanks for offering. I'm sure it'll put Lily's mind at ease to know you're looking out for her."

"You'd do it for our family, Detective."

That was a true statement. "Thank you."

The call was disconnected, and finally, a text from Lily. *Talked to the three witches and brother. Tried to find Alder Perry. No luck. We'll miss lunch.*

I replied. *Alder Perry and Fern Marshall are on the way to the station to be questioned. I'll call Mimi and explain about lunch. Come here, and you can watch.*

She returned a smiley face—*lots to tell you, too. The three weren't upset that Ivy Field had been killed. Ambrose is a mess. He's low on my suspect list but still there. Has an explosive temper. But my amulet got warm around the women, not him. Will save the rest, driving now. XO.*

What did she mean about Ambrose? I didn't text her back since I wanted her to keep her eyes on the road. Even a witch couldn't drive or fly and text.

Chapter 16
Lily

A few hours earlier—

Nikki checked the GPS as I drove down the tree-lined street. She peered through the windshield, squinting against the sun. "It should be on the left, number three."

I slowed the car, put on my blinker, and eased into the driveway. Ahead was a basic black ranch house with a magenta door. The overflowing window boxes were a riot of pink flowers and trailing ivy. Several cars and a pick-up truck were in front of an open garage.

"Looks like they're having a get-together."

I parked the car and wondered if I should leave the keys in the ignition for a quick get-away. But we were two excellent witches, quick with our wands, and we wouldn't let our guard down. I touched my amulet, and it was slightly warm but not alarming. "We should tell them about Ivy Fields and see how they react. From there, I'm going to dive into the two different stories. One, they don't want to be a part of our coven, and the other, fairies and nymphs do."

"Got it." Nikki placed her hand on the door handle and gave me a side glance while keeping an eye in front of us. "Is your wand at the ready?"

"It will be once we get out. I'll slip it down the side of my shorts, and you?"

"Always." She groaned. "We've got company." With a shove, her door flung open, and she jumped out. I did the same.

Violet strode in our direction with Ravena and Morgaine at her heels.

"This is interesting, girls. The newest

leader of the coven has deigned us a visit." She stopped a few feet in front of me. "Didn't your auntie ever tell you it's rude to drop in on another witch?"

"Did that stop you from camping outside my house? And, I might point out, uninvited."

"Look how that turned out for us. One of our best friends is dead." Morgaine took a step closer.

My amulet remained at the same temperature, so I wasn't afraid. "I thought you'd want the most recent news."

Violet's face morphed from annoyed to curious. Her brows arched in twin peaks. "You know who killed Shula?"

"Not yet. But we will soon. It's about your friend, Ivy Fields."

"That nymph is no friend of ours. She and Fern are troublemakers. I don't know why Alder Perry hangs out with them. I guess there's no telling for taste in friends." She cast a look in Nikki's direction. "Are you going to be Lily's right hand?"

Nikki moved her hand to her side, and I knew it rested on the handle of her wand. "We've been best friends for years. New circumstances won't change that."

"Ha." Ravena snorted. "Power goes to a witch's head. We've seen it time and time again."

"Maybe for some, but not Lily."

I appreciated Nikki's quiet but confident demeanor. "We didn't come to talk about anyone's roles in the coven. As I said, it's about Ivy." I paused. I could wait until I had their full attention.

Ravena said, "Come on, Violet. Tell these witches what you think of them."

I leaned against the hood of my car. First, Morgaine stopped grumbling—next, Ravena. Finally, Violet folded her arms behind her back. I would rather have seen her hands if she tried to work up a spell or hex. My fingers grazed my amulet, and it was the same. I pushed the thought of deflecting a spell from my mind since I had never done that before.

"What news?" Ravena and Morgaine bobbed their heads after Violet uttered those two words. It was clear to see who the spokesperson was.

"Ivy Fields was murdered this morning, almost identical to Shula's attack." Not one of them flinched at the news. Had they been expecting it?

"What do you mean by almost identical?" Ravena asked.

"It appears to be the same type of weapon. The attack was from behind her back, and she died quickly."

"Huh. Imagine that." Violet glared at me. "Are you suggesting one of us killed her?"

"I'm not implying anything. But I find it interesting that your stories and the fairies' stories differ on many points—including that you never mentioned Alder, Ivy, and Fern coming to my house and arguing with you."

"Oh, no. They fought with Shula. We stayed out of it. Ivy and Shula had a running feud for years. If you had let us back into the coven, it would have been a big headache for you. Being in charge and all."

Morgaine said, "We thought if we mentioned they had shown up, you'd never listen."

"Do you admit that the disagreement was about being admitted back into the coven?"

The women looked at each other. I got the impression that they understood each other without having to speak, much like Nikki and me.

Violet looked away from her friends. "Look, it's sad that Ivy died. But I won't stand here and pretend to cry over it. She wasn't who others thought her to be. But we never wished her ill will. If we had, we could have used combined magic."

"Part of being a witch is causing no harm to another. Do elemental witches operate by a different value system?"

"I'm not saying we would have killed her. But we could have made her life uncomfortable. She's a wood nymph—we control elements; like fire, water, wind, and earth.

Excessive rain or wind would damage her gardens. That kind of mischief."

"Do you know who would have wanted Shula and Ivy dead? There has to be something connecting the two."

"No." Morgaine said, "Right before they left, Fern hugged Shula, and I heard her say better days were coming."

Nikki, whose hand still rested on the handle of her wand, asked, "Do you know what she meant by that?"

Ravena shook her head. "I wish. Maybe it would help us make sense of what's happened. Until we decided to approach the Pembroke Cove Council, we never had bad luck like this before."

"Maybe it's a curse." Violet's eyes went wide and she pressed the palm of her hand to her chest.

"Who would have cursed you for wanting to have a conversation?" Nikki moved closer to me.

"That would have been something my aunt mentioned yesterday when I heard the news."

"What do you mean about your aunt and yesterday?" Violet's emotions changed rapidly. Now, she was glaring at me again.

"I didn't know I was in line to take over the coven until after discovering Shula's body. My aunt and the council decided I had the right to enjoy my wedding and honeymoon before learning I had a new position waiting for me within the coven."

Ravena narrowed her eyes. "So, if we *had* talked to you, there was nothing you could have done?"

I smiled at the tiny bit of surprise I could spring on them. "That's right. Not until after my wedding."

"We would have looked stupid." A flash of annoyance flitted over Violet's face.

Did that witch ever settle into one mood for longer than thirty seconds? She could be considered volatile in most circumstances. Was it possible she had killed twice?

"Not stupid, but I would have been confused." The last thing I wanted to do was alienate them. Once I oversaw the council, I intended to foster an open dialogue with everyone. With a shake of my head, I wondered if that was possible, considering I didn't know what else I didn't know. At least not yet.

"So, madam, almost-coven-leader, witch. Where do we go from here? Two people are dead. Magical beings must address your council, and you're not even running the coven yet." Ravena threw up her hands. "This is a disaster."

Morgaine said, "Once again, we've jumped the cauldron trying to be first to make change happen."

"That isn't a bad thing. Presumptuous maybe to show up at Lily's before the formal announcement." Nikki said.

"I won't hold that against you. But I need to understand—do the elemental witches want to be a part of the coven again?"

"Yes?" Violet's voice was tentative.

I glanced at Nikki, who nodded. She heard Violet's voice change pitch, too.

"And the other magicals, they too want to rejoin?"

Morgaine spoke up. "Some do. Some don't."

"It's not an all-or-nothing, is it?"

"Your coven, your rules." Violet glanced down the street. "You should go. Ambrose will be here any minute, and he won't be thrilled to find you here."

"I think he'd be pleased to know we're working hard to discover the truth about his sister, and he should know about Ivy, too. From what he said yesterday, he's one of the leaders in Pine Valley."

"Everyone loves Ambrose." Morgaine sighed and rolled her eyes.

Nikki said, "We'll wait."

"It's your neck." Violet strode to the garage, leaving Nikki and I standing in the driveway.

Morgaine tugged on Ravena's dress. "We should go, too."

"You can. I want to hear what these witches tell Ambrose." She cocked a brow. "You should stop doing whatever Violet wants. Change is on the wind, and if there's one thing I know, it's that."

I assumed she meant the element air, but I wasn't about to ask. As Ravena spoke, my amulet had begun to get a little warmer against my skin. A large black jeep skidded to a hard stop, kicking up gravel from oversized tires. I swallowed hard. Ambrose was imposing, but I needed answers to whatever questions popped out of my mouth.

He slammed the driver's door and walked in measured steps to where my car was parked. He looked from Ravena to Morgaine. "Where's Violet?"

Ravena thrust her chin up, and her blue eyes held a glint of steel. "In the garage. Working."

"Maybe you should join her so I can speak freely with our guests."

Morgaine placed her hands on her hips and

assumed what reminded me of the superhero pose. "Not happening. I have just as much right to hear what you'll say as anyone."

He turned his back on the women and gave us a chilly smile. "Lily, Nikki. We haven't been properly introduced." He extended his hand. "Ambrose Ashton."

I shook it while my amulet maintained the same heat level on my skin. He posed little threat as compared to whatever was going on with the others. "Yesterday were trying circumstances for you. I'm so very sorry for your loss."

His skin grew splotchy, and he withdrew his hand. "Thank you. Do you have news?"

"Not about your sister, but earlier this morning, there was another death that we believe is related to Shula's attack." I hated to say murder, it was harsh and unforgiving.

He took two steps closer to me. If I could have backed up, I would have. "What happened?" His voice was curt and his face drawn tight. This was more of a reaction I had expected when we informed the ladies what had happened.

"Ivy Fields was attacked at her home. The coroner believes the weapon used was from the same wood, and the angle was reminiscent of the attack on your sister."

"What are you doing about it?" His voice deepened, and his dark eyes narrowed.

"The police are on the scene."

"Greenleaf, she's a joke. Between her and the junior cop, the best they can do is hand out noise citations and traffic tickets."

"The Pembroke Cove detectives investigating your sister's death are at the scene."

He forced a breath from his lungs. "That's the only reasonable thing I've heard yet. Did they catch the person?" His face paled. "Fern? Was she home? Is she okay?"

"She was, and she's fine. The Chief will find her a place to stay for a few days."

"I have a missed call from Greenleaf. That must be why." He gave a brisk nod. "She can stay with me."

"That's very generous; ultimately, it will be up to Fern where she goes."

His shoulders sagged. "Of course. Lily, do you know why this is happening?"

"I wish I did. Then I could do something to stop it—but I'm not clairvoyant."

"I thought you were powerful. At least we've heard that's why you're assuming your place on the council."

There was so much I could tell Ambrose, but I needed to understand my position better. "May I ask a few questions?"

"Of course, if you think I know something that will help."

"Was there someone who had made threats against either Shula or Ivy recently or in the past?"

"They were friends with extreme opinions, but words were the weapons between them. They had sharp minds and quick outbursts but always hugged it out and never parted angrily."

That was interesting. It meshed with what the others had said about exchanging hugs after the argument. "Is there anyone who wanted to see the meeting between Pine Valley and Pembroke Cove not happen?"

"There will always be a few outliers to any change, but I can say with great confidence that the members of Pine Valley longed to be welcomed back into the fold. After being excluded for several generations, our powers have become weak."

That was interesting. Did they want to come back to plug into the coven's magic? If that was the case, now things were making sense, and I didn't need my clue board for those puzzle pieces.

He turned to Ravena. "Did you tell Lily about your differing opinion with Shula?"

She shifted her weight from one foot to the other. "Well. Um. It's not relevant anymore."

He slowly shook his head. "Everything is relevant until we know who or whom committed these crimes." He spun around. "Tell Lily. Now!"

She held his gaze longer than I thought I

would if I were in her shoes. I didn't like that he was borderline bullying her. "Ambrose. Stop."

In a split second, he went from being a tower of anger to falling to the ground, a sobbing hulk of a man. "I can't bear the thought when my sister needed me most, I failed her. I didn't pick up my phone. That will haunt me for the rest of my days."

I placed a comforting hand on his shoulder and let him cry for what seemed like hours. Ravena and Morgaine dropped to their knees and wrapped their arms around him, murmuring words of support. Finally, he regained his composure. "Find her killer so that she may rest easy."

"I promise you, we will get to the bottom of this." Our next stop was finding Alder Perry. Maybe then we could get a better idea of what happened.

Chapter 17
Lily

Now Nikki's cell pinged with a message. "It's from Mimi. She said she'd dropped lunch off at the station for everyone after Gage messaged her they couldn't get away due to the investigation. Also, she and Nate will close the store today, so you don't need to go in."

"They're saints, and I'm starving." I slowed and turned on Main Street, giving a toot as I drove past my bookstore. "I hope she included cookies or brownies. I could use a sugar pick-me-up."

"Consider it done." Nikki winked and pointed to the back seat.

I had to chuckle. "Sometimes I forget how talented you are. What's in the tins?"

"Your favorites. Blondies and brownies."

I slipped the car into a parking spot outside the police station. Adrenaline rushed through me. "Nikki, this is going to be the turning point. Whatever happens in that building will point us in the right direction of who killed Shula and Fern."

"What makes you so sure?" She plucked the tins of cookies off the back seat.

"I'm not positive. Intuition? Whatever it is, we're close. I can feel it." Opening the car door, I gave her a reassuring look. "No matter what happens or whoever it is, Gage will make sure justice is served."

As we strode up the sidewalk, the sun was mid-point in the bright blue sky. My steps quickened as the door to the station opened.

Gage hurried down and took the tins from Nikki. "Glad you're here. I have Alder in the conference room with Mac. We should hurry. I don't want his nerves to get the best of him so he shuts down."

He held the door, and we sailed through. "How does he seem?"

"Nervous. He and Fern walked in arm and arm. I expected him to be more broken up over Ivy's death. But the two of them are either in shock or great actors."

I tipped my head as I thought of everyone arrested for crimes. "That wouldn't be surprising since we've met quite a few people who've fooled us."

He grimaced. "That's the truth."

I led the way to the observation room. Sharon, Laurel Greenleaf, and EL were inside. "Hello, everyone." I focused my attention on the man sitting with Mac. "That's Alder Perry?"

It was redundant since he couldn't be anyone else, but the room was silent, and it grated on my nerves. I touched my amulet, and it was cool, and offered me comfort. "Gage, ask him who Ivy was dating."

His face scrunched up. "Why?"

"Maybe this has everything to do with jealousy that got out of hand."

"All right, I'll weave it into my questions, but my first point is why Fern, Ivy, and Alder went to the beach after the argument with Shula."

I whipped my head around. "They did?" This was new news. "What else have you discovered?"

He smirked. "Violet, Ravena, and Morgaine disappeared from the security camera footage for almost an hour after they parked the car."

"Which brings our list of suspects back to six," I said more to myself than out loud.

"I'd lean more into Shula's best friends, using that term loosely, than the others."

Sharon asked, "Why? Anyone could be capable, or maybe in some bizarre way, they were all in it together."

EL handed me a few papers. "Lily, look at the report on the weapon."

Sharon inclined her head to the mirror wall. "Mac found her bag, and inside was a note to Ambrose telling him he could do better for a partner; love wasn't the only consideration. He needed to think of the family's future."

"Really?" My voice traveled up an octave. "Did she happen to mention who she thought wasn't right for her brother?"

"That sounds very old-fashioned." Nikki crossed her arms over her chest. "Love shouldn't be cast aside."

I touched her shoulder. "We don't know what happened. With Gage asking questions, maybe we'll get to the bottom of this pretty quickly."

He gave me a peck on my cheek. "If you think of anything I should ask, text me."

I noticed Laurel glaring at me. Were we back to being on opposite sides of the fence? "Chief, do you have something you want to say?"

"I don't get it. You're a bookstore owner. How do you get involved in cases, and the professionals listen to you and go one step further but include you in all aspects of the investigation?"

EL said, "While the police have to stick within specific guidelines, and they're trained to think a certain way, Lily doesn't have those constraints. She and Nikki have helped us look at clues in a different light. They can ask suspects non-threatening but critical questions. Chief, what happens when someone carrying a badge asks questions? Suspects clam up or are so nervous they ramble on about nonsense, and it takes forever to sift through what they've said."

Sharon chimed in, "I was skeptical at first, too. But Lily's mind is razor sharp, and Nikki seems to know how to help her unearth clues. They're a powerful duo."

I didn't know what to say. EL and Sharon's defense lifted my spirits. I had concluded that they accepted me because Gage included me.

However, learning that they respected Nikki and me and considered us valuable team members was the best gift they could have ever given me. I sucked in a quick breath. "Thanks for the support."

Sharon pointed to the mirror. "Gage's about to start."

I sat in a chair close to the mirrored wall. Nikki sat next to me and the rest gathered around. Mac handed Alder Perry a bottle of water. He opened it, took a long drink, and nodded Mac his thanks.

"For the record, please state your name and relationship to the deceased."

Alder placed his hands palms down on the tabletop. "Which one?"

Gage never missed a beat. "Both. Shula Ashton and Ivy Fields."

"I'm Alder Perry. I live in Pine Valley with my dog and two cats. I'm a Forest Preservation Manager for the state. Shula and Ivy were good friends."

"How long had you known the women?"

"We all grew up together from the time our moms took us to play group. Then we went to the same schools."

"Did you get along?"

"Well, yeah, of course we did." He glanced from Gage to Mac and licked his lips before looking at his hands.

Gage remained quiet.

"Like all friends, we occasionally argued, but it wasn't a big deal. More about stupid stuff."

"Like what movie to see?" Mac asked.

Nodding, I said, "And there is our good cop, the kind, friendly guy helping to feed the suspect an answer or two to see where it might lead."

He gave a strained smile to Mac. "Something like that."

"Why were you in Pembroke Cove yesterday?" Gage flipped the pen he was holding and tapped it very quietly on the table.

"I... I..." His shoulders slumped. "How did you know?"

"An eye witness."

"Dang it. I told Ivy we needed to check the area before we went in with guns blazing."

Gage arched a brow. "That's an interesting way of phrasing it."

Alder waved his hand in the air. "That's not what I meant, but Ivy was mad at Shula."

"Not the others?"

"No. They always do what Shula tells them, blindly following the leader." He dropped his head in his hands and moaned. "I can't believe she's dead, and now Ivy, too." He lifted his face and looked from Gage to Mac. "If I tell you something, will you promise not to tell the others?"

Gage never flinched. He wasn't one to make promises he wouldn't keep but wouldn't jeopardize an investigation. He'd use whatever information he had to get a full confession. "I can keep your name out of this."

He looked to Mac, who nodded. "You can trust Detective Erikson."

He swallowed. I saw his Adam's apple bob

in his neck. The seconds ticked, and Gage sat patiently. Mac fidgeted in his chair, seemingly uncomfortable in the silence like it was a ploy.

"Shula called me a couple of days ago after they decided to come to Pembroke Cove and try to speak with Lily Michaels."

I cringed, hoping he wouldn't use the word witch, coven, or council in his following statement. "Shula said that soon Lily was going to be in charge of an organization she and Morgaine wanted to join, but Violet and Ravena didn't." I still held my breath. He must realize there could be non-magicals anywhere.

"I don't understand why the conflict." Gage remained casual in his posture.

I leaned forward. This might be critical to the investigation.

"They, or we've, always done everything together. If two wanted to join and the others didn't, it would cause a division in the group."

Laurel muttered under her breath, but I couldn't hear what she said.

Mac said, "People have the right to choose what they want to do."

Alder shook his head. "Not according to Shula, or Ambrose, for that matter. All for one and that nonsense."

I wondered if we'd need to bring Ambrose back in for questioning. Maybe now he could shed some light on the new situation.

"Did Ivy agree with her? Is that why they argued?"

"They weren't arguing with each other. Ivy was supporting Shula's points, and I thought we got through to them, and we were all in agreement that each," he looked at Gage, "everyone could decide for themselves, and Ambrose would just have to deal."

I glanced at Laurel and dropped my voice so that Sharon couldn't hear what I was about to ask. "It sounds like Ambrose oversees the council. Did you know any of this?"

She stepped back as her gaze darted between me and Alder. "We don't have an official council. Not like here. There's just been an understanding of how things run. I'm around to ensure no one gets out of line, and it's worked for decades. Why change it now?"

Sharon glanced over as Laurel's voice grew louder while discussing change. At least she hadn't paid attention to our back and forth. "It's part of life. Can you imagine if everything stayed the same forever?"

Laurel gave a short, dismissive laugh as she focused on me. "Sometimes change isn't all that it's purported to be."

I couldn't rise to the bait in here; she knew that. Jabbing at me was a perk for her.

"Lily, do you disagree with me?" She arched a brow in challenge.

Sharon looked from me to Laurel and then glanced at EL. Nikki turned in her chair and placed her hand on my shoulder. "I don't think this is the time to discuss how an organization chooses to run. We should pay more attention to what's happening as Gage questions a murder suspect and put any posturing aside for another time."

Laurel lifted one shoulder. "Suit yourself, but Lily knows I'm right."

I turned my back on her, confident that would speak volumes and better than words could.

"Tell me why you went to the beach. And how long after the ladies left did you follow? Was it planned to meet up, leaving Shula alone?"

"There was no plan. We started heading back to Pine Valley when Fern and Ivy said it would be nice to take a detour and dip their toes in the water. We don't come over this way often. I was happy to oblige. I thought it would be a good way to wash away the negativity of meeting the others."

"Did you see them when you got to the beach?"

He said, "No. I saw their car. I don't remember seeing them anywhere when we walked down the wooden slats to the water. But they could have been in the ladies' room. That was the reason they left Shula."

"Did the three of you stay together?" Gage leaned forward slightly.

"No. I went for a swim. Fern and Ivy said they were going to look for shells. We agreed to meet up in an hour and go home."

"And did you?"

"Of course. The water was refreshing. Fern and Ivy were waiting for me when I got back to the car."

"Did they have shells?"

I stood up. My hand was against the mirrored glass as I held my breath. This was a crucial piece of new information.

His face crumpled. "Now that you ask, they didn't have shells or even sand on their feet."

They were never close enough to the water to carry sand back to the car. I twirled around. "EL. Did you run fingerprints on the weapon that killed Shula against Ivy and Fern?"

"I asked Sharon for a consult, and we're waiting for the results, but not Ivy, just Fern, Ambrose, Violet, Ravena, and Morgaine." His eyes grew wide. "Are you thinking what I think you're thinking?"

"Yes. Can you do that right away? I know there are a lot of subtleties when it comes to fingerprints, but if you can get a close match, it would help. There should be two different sets."

"I'll make a couple of calls and check the results here."

"Good. Also, can you check on the handbag? Mac logged it into evidence but hasn't mentioned it since. Why did someone hide it? There must be something important inside the bag."

Sharon looked from EL to me. Laurel stepped closer, and I texted Gage.

Before you talk to Fern, I need to see you.

I watched as he glanced at his phone and gave a slight nod. I knew who killed Ivy and Shula. All we needed to do was wait for fingerprint evidence and Gage could extract a confession with the right line of questioning.

Laurel said, "There is no way that Fern killed those women."

"Did I say that she did?" I wasn't about to share my theory with the police chief, who obviously didn't think much of my problem-solving method.

"Nikki, I'm going to get drinks. Would you set up lunch?" I hoped she'd see through me that I needed to talk to Gage alone, and feeding people kept them occupied. We needed a strategy to close this case.

"Um. Sure, if everyone's hungry, Mimi brought over a ton of food, and I baked some bar cookies."

My back was to the group except for her and I mouthed *thank you* before heading to Gage's office.

Within minutes, he strode in and closed the door. I cast a quick spell so if anyone lingered outside, they couldn't overhear us. I gestured to his clue board and smiled. "Not bad."

"Thanks. It's nothing like yours would be, but this case has been moving at the speed of light. There hasn't been time for you to do your thing." He kissed my cheek. "What do you have?"

"Okay, I'm either way off base or dead on. So, how you interview Fern could tip the scales in our favor. But one thing I am sure of; one person killed Shula, and someone else killed Ivy, but the same motive drove them."

Chapter 18
Gage

As Lily told me her hypothesis, I had to agree it was plausible. "If I approach Fern with this line of questions, do you think she'll confess?"

Lily added the detail of Fern and Ivy looking for shells but no sand and Alder going for a swim. "That's the hope."

I crossed the office and put my hand on the doorknob. "Are you going back to the observation room?"

"Yes. But," I could see Lily chewing on the

corner of her lip. "Why do you think this case is going so fast? Don't you find it odd?"

"It *is* unusual, but these suspects are all magical in one way or another. It might be influencing this investigation." I walked away from the door, closing the distance between us. "Are you concerned I'll arrest the wrong person?"

She shook her head. "No. I believe you'll get a confession out of the guilty party." A tap on the door caused her to jump. "You'd better get that. It could be important."

The door swung wide. Peabody was in the hall. "Detective, I thought you'd want to know that Violet Bradford, Ambrose Ashton, Morgaine Waterson, and Ravena Erikson showed up and demanded to speak with you."

"Any idea on the specifics?"

She shook her head. "I asked, but Mr. Ashton said he'd only speak with you."

I gave her a curt nod. This was a wrinkle I hadn't been expecting. "I'll be right out. Have them wait in the lobby."

"You got it."

I made sure the door was firmly closed. "Lily, with so much of this case tied to magic and witches, how will I handle that when these people start talking? The explanation of you being in charge of a group without confirming what that group is has made Mac curious. He gave me that pensive look he gets when he thinks I'm not fully disclosing information."

"I've thought about what will happen when one of our suspects starts talking about petitioning the coven to rejoin. The only way we can head that off is to either say they're confused or cast a spell on Sharon and Mac that they hear certain words differently if they come up."

I rubbed the back of my neck. "I don't want to lie to them or find a way to skirt the truth. Integrity is too important to me."

"We can't be honest with them unless EL's already told Sharon." She frowned. "I can ask him, but you know the entire premise of our council is that we remain a secret in plain sight.

I don't know what would happen if we brought them into the circle of knowledge."

I couldn't help but smile a little. "Is that what the council calls it?"

She shook her head. "Nope. It just popped out."

"I like it."

"Thanks. I'll call Aunt Mimi to see if she can provide some direction regarding Sharon and Mac. One of these people is going to say the word witch or coven. It's just a matter of time."

"Now that the others have arrived, I agree." I opened the door and gestured for Lily to walk ahead of me. I tugged her hand as she passed. "I know I don't say this often, but thank you for helping me with cases. Not only do you help solve the crimes quicker, but I like how well we work together."

She cupped my cheek and smiled. "We make a great team and not just solving murder."

Ambrose paced the lobby while the women sat in chairs. He abruptly stopped when he saw me standing in the doorway. "Detective Erikson." His voice was flat and his eyes vacant. He was the picture of grief walking. "When I heard you brought Fern and Alder in for questioning, I couldn't wait at home for an update. I had to come."

"I understand, but there isn't much I can share with you now." The women's eyes were locked on us.

He hung his head. "The ladies wanted to come. I thought it might be a good idea since Violet mentioned she had never told you about yesterday's argument between everyone."

"It's good that you're all here. It will save time if I need to question any of you again."

Violet jumped off the chair as if it was on fire. "What do you mean, question us again? We would never have harmed Shula. She was one of us."

Did she mean as a witch and part of their coven or as their friend? "Then why didn't you mention Shula argued with Ivy or even that Fern, Alder, and Ivy were with you?"

"I" Color flushed her cheeks. "You think Ivy hurt Shula, but she wouldn't have. It had to be a stranger, someone driving by who saw that she was alone on the side of the road."

"There would be no motive." I shouldn't be having this conversation in the middle of the lobby, but in their emotional state, something might slip out. I never took my eyes off Violet as she stole glances at Ravena and Morgaine, who remained silent.

Ambrose stepped in between me and the women. "Are you questioning Alder and Fern now?"

I saw no reason to withhold the information. "Yes. You can wait here."

"Ask Fern why Shula and Ivy disagreed about talking to Lily." He inclined his head slightly to the three women huddled together. "They won't tell you the truth unless it serves them somehow. Fern will. She's as honest as the sun rising in the east."

"Thank you." I turned away and strode down the hall. His comment was in direct contradition to Lily's theory. At this point, I was close to getting a confession from one of my suspects. I could feel it like an incoming hurricane.

Fern Marshall was in a conference room. Peabody was with her when I walked in and closed the door. The small green light blinked in the corner, which indicated it was recording, and the speaker was on in the observation room. I glanced at the mirrored wall. Even though I couldn't see Lily, I felt her calming presence.

The chair's legs grated over the linoleum floor as I sat across from Fern.

"I'm very sorry for what you've been through today. Losing someone close to us is hard, almost unbearable when it's violent."

She shuddered. "Yes." Her voice quivered, and she drew her arms closer to her body as if she wanted to disappear. "I'll never have another friend like Ivy." She lifted her tear-drenched face. "You will get her, won't you?"

I tipped my head as she used the word, her.

"Get who?" I hoped she was referring to who she thought killed Shula and Ivy.

She wiped her cheeks on the hem of her tee shirt. "One of those witches killed Ivy, and you should arrest all three of them until the guilty person confesses."

I needed to compose my next question carefully. "Tell me about the argument yesterday. Why did you, Ivy, and Alder follow the others to Lily Michaels's house?"

She glanced at Peabody and shrugged. "They were determined to talk to Lily about joining her group. You know the one she's going to be running soon." She darted a glance at Peabody and back to me. "It's been a sensitive subject in our group for six months. Some of us like things the way they are. Laid back, we keep to ourselves, and enjoy life. Others want to enrich their," she hesitated, "capacity to be better at," she paused again, "things."

"Who wanted what?" Peabody's brows knitted together as she gave me a questioning glance. I stayed focused on Fern.

"I'm sure you can guess, but Shula and friends wanted to join, and Alder, me, and Ivy didn't."

Peabody cleared her throat. "You have a choice to be a part of what you want, and you don't need anyone's permission."

Fern clasped her hands together, and her knuckles were white. "No. It's like a union. All for one and one for all." Her chin dropped to her chest. "Ivy thought if she could talk to Shula, who was the spokesperson for Pine Valley, she could convince her to wait until after your wedding. It would give our side time to gain support for why we wanted to stay independent."

"So this issue divided the town?" Laurel should have told me this right away. I wouldn't say I liked learning this tidbit from a suspect.

Fern's breath came faster as her chest heaved. "Yes. It's never been this bad before. Things come up in town, and we've always found a way to compromise. That didn't happen this time. Now Shula and Ivy are dead, and there's a murderer on the loose." Her face went from pale to horror-stricken. "Do you think she'll kill me, too? For talking to you?"

"No one's going to hurt you." Peabody placed a comforting hand on her shoulder. "I promise."

Tears coursed unchecked down Fern's cheeks. "I never thought something like this would happen to people I knew and cared about."

"Were you and Shula friends, too?"

"Not really. She and Ivy were great friends. But those other witches won't tell you that. Violet was the ringleader of those three, and she didn't like us. She said we were goody two shoes and never wanted to have any fun."

"What about Ambrose?"

Her eyes softened. "He's not like that at all. He thinks everyone has a special place in our community."

Could she have feelings for him? Was that relevant to this investigation? "Are you two close?"

Her eyes flew open, and her cheeks flushed crimson. "Gosh, no. He and Morgaine have been dating forever."

"How did Shula and Morgaine get along?"

"They've been best friends our whole lives. Morgaine doesn't show much emotion, but her feelings are like a deep underground river. You have no idea how powerful it is while it's wearing away rocks."

That was an interesting analogy. But she was a water witch if I was to go by her last name. "Can you think of any reason someone would want to hurt Shula other than the division you mentioned?"

"No. It had to have been someone just passing by. Besides, she had everything she wanted to say written down and stashed it in her bag just in case she got nervous speaking to the great Lily Michaels."

I leaned across the table, and she shrank back. "What about Ivy? Surely, you don't think it's a coincidence. Two people lost their lives within twenty-four hours. Why don't you think they're connected?" I stared at her. "Is it possible that someone knew both the women and killed one and then the other because of yesterday's argument?"

She pressed her eyes tight together, and her lips trembled. Shaking her head, she whimpered. "No."

"Yes."

She opened her eyes and, in a strangled whisper, said, "One of my friends killed a friend and then my best friend. That's not possible."

"Most all murders are committed by someone who is known to the victim. The idea these attacks were random is virtually impossible."

"But," she looked to Peabody for support. "Violet said it had to be someone that didn't know us."

"When did you speak with Violet?"

"Last night. We got together to support each other. Shula is the first person in our group to..."

"I understand." Now it was time to be brutal. "Fern, did you kill Shula or Ivy by stabbing them in the back?"

Her hand flew to her mouth, and she cried, "No. I won't even kill an ant. That's not how I was raised. In my family, kindness is everything for all living creatures." This time, she dissolved into hysterics.

Peabody looked at me, and I felt terrible for pushing Fern to the breaking point, but this was a serious matter. I looked at the glass, wondering what Lily was thinking. In my mind, unless Fern was a complete fake, she didn't kill either woman. I needed the fingerprint report on the weapon, and then I'd wrangle a confession from the guilty party. Someone in this building killed those women.

My chair screeched across the floor as I stood. "Fern, can I get you a water or coffee?"

"Water." Her voice sounded parched. More than likely due to all the tears she had shed.

I nodded to Peabody, who returned the gesture. When I stepped out of the room, Lily emerged from the observation area.

"Thoughts?"

Her lips were flat, and she showed no emotion. "EL texted. He wants to see us in your office."

"Maybe this is the break we need."

She walked ahead of me, placed her finger over her lips, and then circled her index finger in front of her. She wanted me to remain quiet until we reached my office so she could cast another spell to block out everyone.

EL was striding down the hall in our direction. He closed the door once we were inside and handed me a tablet. "The preliminary results we've been waiting for."

Before I looked at the information, I had to know. "How accurate is it?"

"Ninety-five percent. Once you scan the report and while we're in here, you'll need to develop a line of questions to draw out the real killer."

"Why do I get the feeling this is not what we were expecting?"

He shook his head. "It's not what I thought. I was in the camp that one of the witches committed both murderers."

I scanned the report and handed it to Lily. When she was done, she handed it back to EL. "Well, this certainly changes everything, and I'm going to say, I'm shocked. One set of prints. I didn't see that coming."

"Me either." I perched on the edge of my desk. "What do you think is the best way to approach a confession?"

Tapping her finger to her lips, her eyes widened. "I've got it. We put them all in one room together. For safety we'll need to have Laurel agree to the plan. Before we do, I need to talk with Nikki and EL. This isn't an ordinary group of suspects. We must be prepared to contain the situation when spells start to fly."

"Is this going to be dangerous?" I was out of my element here. Without magic to defend anyone, I needed to rely on my favorite witch.

She took my hand and gave it a reassuring squeeze. "There is the potential, more from Ambrose than anyone else."

"Do what you need to do, and let me know when I should bring everyone into the main conference room. You'll tell me what questions I should ask unless you're comfortable asking them yourself." I didn't phrase it as a question because it was a statement to remind myself that we were in this together. I gave her a bear hug.

"As the almost new head of the coven, I'd like to handle this. But if you feel the need to jump in, please do."

"Lily, please promise you'll be extra careful."

She hugged me tight. "Witches' honor."

Chapter 19
Lily

Nikki and EL were on opposite sides of the conference room. I briefly considered Mac and Peabody being exposed to magic, but we had no choice. Making a bold move was the only way to flush out the real murderer.

With Laurel's assistance, Gage ushered the six suspects into the room, which contained a large rectangular table surrounded by fourteen chairs, even though we had an unlucky thirteen people present. "Take a seat, everyone. We," his gaze traveled around the room, drawing us all into that *we*, "think it's best if we lay our cards on the table."

Ambrose stood at one end and nodded.

Everyone did as Gage requested and sat down. Sharon, Mac, and EL sat together. Facing the six suspects who hadn't flinched. Instead, they casually glanced at each other. This is like the scene in which Hercule Poirot lines everyone up at the end of the book *Murder on the Orient Express.*

Gage stood at the unoccupied end. He pressed his knuckles into the table and his voice sliced the room. "Do you know how hard it is to uncover the truth in any crime when everyone lies?"

Silence blanketed the room like a thick, wet fog. My hand rested against my lower back, and my fingertips were on the hilt of my wand.

Ravena looked at her friends. "We've told you the truth, Detective."

"Have you? Only one person at this table mentioned Ivy, Fern, and Alder were at the beach while Violet's car was parked there, but you ladies weren't anywhere to be found."

Violet folded her hands together on the tabletop. "What are you talking about? We used the restroom and got some sea air and salt water before returning to Lily's."

"Did you see Alder, Ivy, and Fern?"

"No. They weren't there." Violet glared at Fern.

I tapped the remote for the large screen and waited while it slowly descended from the ceiling. "Maybe we should look at the footage from the beach cams."

Ravena shifted in her chair and bit her lower lip. "We've got nothing to hide."

I kept my eye on the group as Sharon rolled the security footage.

Gage said, "As you can see, Violet parks the car here, and you three get out and walk around the building. That's the last time you're seen for at least forty-five minutes. Did you spend that entire time in the bathhouse?" Gage held up his hand. "No need to answer that just yet." He fast-forwarded the footage. "Here we see Alder, Ivy, and Fern arrive. After they park, the ladies go in one direction, per Alder, to gather shells. He goes to the water for a swim. Fern, would you tell us how many shells you gathered and why you didn't have sand on your feet when you returned to the car?"

"Ivy and I had a disagreement, and we never looked for shells. Instead, we walked out to the road and talked."

I relaxed my hand on my wand. It was comforting to have it ready, but I didn't need it to cast a protection spell. I asked, "What did you argue about?"

"Shula. She almost had Ivy convinced to abandon Alder and me and our ways."

"And after you walked, did she agree to stand with you?"

"Yes and no. She wanted to be a part of the larger conversation with you. I mean, I understood, and I was worried that she'd side with Shula, but Alder can be very persuasive."

My gaze slid to him. "You didn't know they were arguing when you went for a swim?"

He leaned the chair back on two legs. "Nope."

Fern glared at him. "Yes, you knew. We argued from Lily's street to the beach."

"You two are always bickering. I ignored what it was about." He studied his fingernails and chewed on what I guessed was a hangnail.

"Morgaine, you've been quiet. What did you observe during the argument between Shula and Ivy?"

"Nothing out of the ordinary. Just two friends with a difference of opinion."

I crossed my arms over my mid-section. "Then why did you bury your handbag in the leaves?"

"I didn't." She glanced at Fern.

Alder dropped the chair to four legs. "What did you do?"

With a smug smile, Fern avoided him. "Nothing. What are you guilty of, Morgaine?

Leaving your bag behind so you could circle back and talk with Lily yourself?"

"No. That would have been counterproductive, especially after Shula died. There's no way I could have stashed anything, let alone my bag. Shula asked me to take *her* bag with me. I thought she was being over-sensitive, but I did it anyway."

Gage cleared his throat. "Morgaine's right. She didn't bury it. Our killer thought it was Shula's. When they buried it, they thought they were hiding evidence."

"Because the killer believed Shula when she said she had documents to support her claim to be reinstated into the, er, club." I glanced at Nikki, and she gave me an encouraging smile.

Morgaine leveled her gaze at me. "When did she say that?"

"Why would anyone be stupid enough to do that?" Ravena licked her lips and looked from Violet to Morgaine.

Ambrose leveled his gaze on Ravena. "What do you know about Shula's bag?"

His deep voice caused my belly to rumble, and he wasn't questioning me.

Gage said, "We believe they thought Shula's notes were in the bag and didn't look." He turned to Ravena. "Do you have them?"

"Who, me?"

Ambrose slammed his fists on the table. "I've had enough of this tap dancing." He glared at Gage. "Do you know who killed my sister or not?"

"We do, and we know who killed Ivy Fields, in case that interests anyone." Gage stood, feet planted on the floor. He didn't look at anyone other than Ambrose. "Your friends have yet to tell the truth about what happened yesterday. It's getting late, and I'm sure we're all anxious to get to the bottom of this, so we have two choices. We can continue this conversation, or I can lock the six of you up for the night, hospitality compliments of the Pembroke Cove Police Department."

"Detective, might I have a word?" Laurel finally said something. I wondered how effective she was as the chief when she had deferred the entire case to Gage and his team. Ever since she arrived with Fern and Alder, she had remained silent, not once asking if she could question anyone.

I caught his eye. Before he broke contact, he lifted a brow in that questioning manner. If he needed to appease Laurel, he might as well do it.

"Mac, you're with me." Gage strode out the door with Mac, and Laurel followed them.

Here was a golden opportunity. Sharon was present but hadn't said anything, so maybe the suspects weren't paying attention to her.

The moment the door closed, I rubbed my hands together. "Now that the detectives have left the room, let's get down to it, shall we?" I pulled over a rolling chalkboard. If Peabody wondered where it came from, she never batted an eyelash.

I wrote Shula and Ivy's names in the

middle and circled them. "We have two victims of murder with the same kind of weapon. A piece of yew wood that was shaped and sharpened into a dagger. We learned from the medical examiner that the wood was cut from the same tree. Those details on how he came to that conclusion aren't important." I scanned the group of people studying me. "Any questions so far?"

Ambrose sat down and crossed his ankle over his knee. "Continue."

"The four ladies came to my house around eleven yesterday. After picnicking on the side of the road, Ivy, Fern, and Alder showed up. An argument ensued about whether I should be approached about joining the groups from Pine Valley and Pembroke Cove. After agreeing to be on different sides of the argument, did you all part as friends?" I let that question hang in the air.

Alder said, "Basically, we agreed to disagree, and Shula said she would consider waiting to speak with you. That was good enough for us, so we left."

Fern nodded. "And we went to the beach. After all, we were so close it'd be a shame not to."

"But you mentioned that you and Ivy were still arguing. The two of you and Alder went in different directions. Along with our missing trio."

Violet said, "If we had wanted to hurt Shula, do you think we would have brought her to Pembroke Cove only to murder her in front of your house? Talk about stupid."

I jabbed the chalk in her direction. "So tell me where the three of you went once you got to the beach? You don't have an alibi, and it would be pretty easy for one of you, or all, to circle back to my place. The walk isn't that far, and you could have stuck to the trees to avoid anyone seeing you."

Ambrose's face flushed beet red as he drew himself up taller. "Are you saying my sister's best friends joined forces to murder her?"

"Ambrose, this is hard for you, but please allow me to continue." If he had doubts, I could push out the confession. He seemed willing to defer to me.

Violet said, "All right, we ditched the car but didn't go to your house. There's a part of Pine Valley that would be a great place to have a spa. The land would need to be cleared of trees. But the location is ideal—close to the ocean but tucked back. I wanted to get pictures for the proposal."

Alder kicked his chair back and stood. "What parcel?"

Now we were getting somewhere.

She smirked at him. "The Grove, just outside of Pembroke Cove."

He slapped his hand on the table. "You promised me that you'd look at other areas. That land is sacred to my kind."

I held up my hand. "What are you talking about?"

Alder turned to me. "My family has been stewards of that land for generations. We had an argument when Shula first bought the land and then brought up the idea of razing it for a stupid spa. Yesterday, she mentioned it again, but I...”

Violet laughed as she cut him off mid-sentence. “You knew Shula lied to you on the spot. I watched your face morph from anger to livid. Your nostrils flared just like they’re doing now.”

His eyes turned cold and hard, almost flint like. He smacked the table again. “You think you’re so smart. Outwitting the dumb wood nymph. I told Shula she’d have that land for a commercial business over my dead body. But as luck would have it, she’s dead, and before she died, she turned ownership over to me.”

Violet’s brow drew together. “What do you mean before she,” her hand flew to her mouth. Peabody put herself between Violet and Alder as he scrambled over the table, his hands outstretched to wrap around her throat. He knocked Sharon aside. She hit the concrete wall with a snap as if she were nothing more than a twig.

"Nikki, help her."

EL was kneeling next to her limp form. At least Sharon had foiled Alder's attempt at strangling Violet. Instead, he grabbed Morgaine. Her eyes were wide with fear as his hands tightened around her arm, jerking her to him.

Using Morgaine as a human shield, he started to walk backward toward the door.

"Alder, you have no place to go."

His eyes were wild, and he withdrew a dagger from what seemed like thin air. Holding it aloft, he said, "Don't come any closer."

Ambrose hissed. "Do something. You're the great one."

I ignored him. I wanted Alder to focus on me, and I could get Morgaine from his grasp without harming anyone. "Alder, it's okay. No one will do anything to The Grove, but we should talk about what really happened yesterday."

My amulet burned against my chest. He pointed the dagger, now more like a wand, toward the door, and a satisfied look filled his wild eyes. "Did you know I've learned to be a formidable opponent with magic despite our reputation?"

I asked, "That's how you got the jump on Shula."

He nodded toward Ravena. "I asked her for the wind to wipe away the anger from where we fought. She was happy to comply."

I remembered the breeze had been unnaturally strong for this time of year. I should have paid closer attention.

"Ravena, you always were so trusting when it came to me. I used the sound of the wind to hide my approach," he said.

I moved so that I was between everyone but Alder and Morgaine. "Sneaking up on her is a better way to describe it. Did you argue again?"

Alder's eyes were cold as he glared at me. "Aren't you a brilliant witch? Maybe everyone is right, and you are the right person to run the coven into the next century. However, Morgaine and I won't be around to witness it firsthand."

"Alder, wait. Tell me what happened," I said.

His face screwed up. "I handed her the paper to sign the land over to me. She didn't want to, but I promised her I'd help convince you of whatever Shula wanted. I can be very persuasive when necessary."

I knew I had to keep pressing him for answers. "And then?"

He held up the dagger in his hand. "I had another one of these. She started to taunt me about always hugging trees. I don't remember how it happened, but I plunged the yew dagger in and ran."

My brows knitted together, "Why did you kill Ivy?" One confession down. One to go.

He raised the dagger, ready to plunge it into Morgaine. I hastily cast a protection spell around her.

With his arm raised, he said, "Ivy figured it all out, and after we got together last night, I knew she'd tell on me." His voice had gotten childlike, almost feminine. That tone was what Fern heard outside the house.

He continued, "If she told the truth, the land wouldn't be protected. The rights would go to Ambrose, not me. When I went to her house this morning, I knew Fern was in the kitchen, but I needed to talk to Ivy. When she saw me, she said I had to turn myself in."

I softened my voice as I tried to sound like a friend. "Alder, now you can, and it will be all over."

He brought the dagger down in a slicing motion. I was surprised when it wasn't in Morgaine's direction but in mine. I put my left arm up in self-defense and felt the burn of the dagger as it sliced my skin. Inwardly, I groaned; that was going to leave a mark.

In a flash, I withdrew my wand. I didn't recognize the spell as the words rang out. *"Root this nymph like a tree to protect him and me."*

Ambrose was advancing on us. I extended my bloodied arm.

I continued, *"No harm will come to anyone*

within this room, and forgiveness must now bloom. For this I wish, so it shall be."

I heard Gage frantically banging on the door. "Lily, let me in."

EL and Nikki shielded the others while I focused on Alder. "You have to confess to Detective Erikson."

Alder hung his head, a defeated nymph. "I'm sorry." He gestured toward my arm. "The resin I use on the daggers will make you extremely sick; if you wait too long, it could be fatal."

With a flick of my wrist, I unlocked the door. Gage burst in with Laurel close behind.

"Gage, honey, you can arrest Alder. Ambrose and the ladies were witnesses to his confession. I need to find Aunt Mimi." I held up my arm as the room started to waver.

His face blanched when he saw the blood. In two steps, he had slipped a supportive arm around my waist.

EL sat Sharon up in a chair as her eyes fluttered. He said, "Don't worry, I know what it is, and Mimi can handle it."

Gage briefly took control. "Mac, arrest Alder and get everyone's statements." We took two steps toward the door, and I stumbled.

"Nikki, call Aunt Mimi and tell her we'll be at the bookstore in a few minutes."

She had her phone out and was already talking.

"Gage, will you still marry me if I have an ugly scar?"

He chuckled softly and half-carried, half-walked me through the lobby and down the station steps before he swept me off my feet. He pressed his lips to my cheek as we made our way across the town square. "As if that could stop me."

Chapter 20
Lily

A heavy weight pressed into the middle of my chest as I opened my eyes.

"Finally, I can see your baby browns." Milo purred loudly. "I was wondering if you were going to sleep the day away. We've got a lot to do."

I lifted him to a pillow and pushed myself to a half-sitting position. My left arm ached, and I glanced at the bandage. It was completely white, so that was a good sign. "Can't we ease into the morning? The last two have been pretty intense."

"I know. Who would have ever thought you'd unmask a killer only on day two of the investigation? That has to be a record!"

My fingers ruffled the fur on his neck. "It was a group effort, and the whole situation was sad. If I had been home, maybe all of this could have been avoided." I shook my head. "Milo, is this what I have to look forward to when I oversee the council?"

"Of course not. This was a one-off, and after the wedding, you'll see. That coven will be in great hands, ours."

I laughed and pulled his warm body to my chest, kissing the top of his head. "Milo, you're the best familiar."

"I know. Now," he wriggled from my arms and walked over my legs, "get dressed. Everyone's going to be here to talk about the case over breakfast, and then we can move on to getting us married to Detective Cutie."

The door nudged open and Gage stepped in carrying two mugs of coffee. "Good morning, sweetheart. I thought you could use a small incentive."

I held out my hands. "I could get used to this."

He grinned. "Noted."

I took a first sip and let the heat flow through me. I tipped my head. "Did you add something to this?"

"Per your aunt's directions." He sat next to me. "I'm not one to disregard Mimi Michaels O'Brien."

I took another sip. "Smart man."

Milo rubbed against Gage's leg. "My dear witch, your detective has grown on me. You have my official blessing to marry the big lug."

I gave him an indulgent smile but didn't respond. It was useless explaining to my future husband that it had taken Milo all these years to realize what I had known most of my life.

Gage said, "Here's what I'm thinking."

I took his hand and grimaced as a painful reminder of yesterday throbbed. "Tell me."

He kissed the bandage. "Does it hurt that bad?"

"It's better now, and I'm sure when Aunt Mimi checks it today, it will be almost as good as new." I flashed a bright smile just for him. But I did have questions about whatever was on that dagger or whatever it was.

"Nikki and Steve will be here shortly, and she's bringing breakfast for everyone. The gang will arrive in thirty minutes, give or take. I figured one final conversation about the two cases, and we can move on to wedding festivities. After all, we're getting married in three days."

A shiver of happy anticipation raced over me. He kissed my lips. "Take your time getting ready." He pointed at my cup. "Drink all of that before your feet touch the floor, and don't be snarky to the messenger; that is a direct order from the current head of the Pembroke Cove coven."

I held up my hands in a playful surrender. "I'd never go against her orders." I pointed to the door. "Go be the host, and I'll be out soon."

Brutus lumbered into the room, crawled onto the bed, and lay down as close as he could to Milo. Gage stroked his head. "I see where your allegiance lies, old man."

Milo asked, "Doesn't he get the familiar–witch connection yet?"

"He's not *my* familiar, he's attached to Milo."

Gage snorted. "Traitor."

Milo grumbled. "Tell him around here we're a family and not to be jealous."

I hid a snicker behind my hand and put on my poker face. "Gage, Milo wants you to know that we're a family. Oh, and he wants Brutus as your best four-legged baby in the wedding, just like Milo will be mine."

"No. I'm your best familiar, and Brutus is the ring bearer, and we're wearing bowties." He hopped down and muttered, "I'd better see what Nikki's cooking. With any luck, there'll be some smoked salmon."

Gage did a double take. "Milo wants Brutus to be a part of our wedding?"

"He does; in fact, he's insistent they wear matching bow ties."

His voice trembled. "Well, call me shocked. The little man really has accepted us." He kissed his fingertips and blew it in my direction. "Coffee first, love." He closed the door.

I walked into the kitchen, and the conversation ended.

"Hey, everyone."

Sharon crossed the room and took my left hand. She studied the bandage and then looked at me. "You were attacked because of me."

"I got hurt because someone who was very confused lashed out at people I care about, so I did what I had to do to protect them, including you."

EL said, "Lily, I've tried to tell her that, but she blames herself."

I wrapped my arms around her and held her tight. Nikki came over and wrapped her arms around us both. She said, "Sharon, you put yourself between Alder and Violet. You protected her, which was your job. I saw that murderous look in his eyes, and you were fearless."

She exhaled as her body trembled. "I wasn't able to help Lily."

"How could you? Alder tossed you into that wall and knocked you out." I ran my hand down her back, attempting to soothe her. "It's over, and he's behind bars. That's all that matters."

Sharon stepped back and looked me in the eye. "Thank you. When Flora Gray was killed, I was annoyed at you poking your nose into police business, but now I'm glad you did."

"I'm proud to call you my friend, Sharon."

Gage steered me to a chair. "Let's get the case discussion behind us so we can talk about the wedding. I, for one, am looking forward to calling this woman my wife and having a huge party on the beach."

Steve chimed in, "It's about time, too."

Aunt Mimi and Nate made a grand entrance with a tray of cinnamon pecan buns, croissants, and muffins. "Compliments of William and the Sweet Spot."

Gage took the tray from Nate and kissed Mimi's cheek. "Lily's having some pain with her arm. Will you check it out?"

She patted her tote bag. "Everything I need is right in here."

I hugged Nate and then Aunt Mimi. "You're just in time. We were going to review the case again, and then it's all about the wedding."

She laughed, "My timing has always been impeccable, except once at the library." She winked at me. It was funny how Sharon had just brought up the same case.

My plate was piled high with quiche, bacon, and, of course, a pecan cinnamon bun.

I set my fork aside. "I've been thinking about Alder and why he killed Shula and Ivy."

Sharon sipped her coffee. "I thought it was odd when we initially were told it had something to do with your book club, Lily. Not that everyone camping outside your house still makes any sense, but if his family felt such a strong connection to The Grove, I can understand why he was passionate about land preservation. I agree with the ladies; a spa would be heaven—so we don't have to drive to Portland."

I thought it was cute that Sharon decided *my club* was a book club since we never specified anything. That made things easier. "I'm not sure it was as much about Shula going against what the residents of Pine Valley or Alder's family wanted. Ambrose said she loved to tease Alder. I think he took her at her word, and when she wouldn't let up, things escalated to the point where he lost control."

EL beamed with pride at Sharon. "I asked Sharon to look at the prints on the weapon, and her input connected the two sets. Something about that resin made the comparison more difficult."

"Fingerprints were my thing before I moved to town. I was happy to help. But there's something I don't understand. Why did Alder kill Ivy? They were close."

Aunt Mimi refilled coffee cups in a non-magical way. "That *is* puzzling. Weren't they cousins?"

I knew she was asking if they were both nymphs. "No, Ivy and Fern were related." Since there was no way to clarify who a nymph or fairy was, I left that comment there.

"Oh." Aunt Mimi retook her seat. "This all boils down to anger taking control over a plot of land. When will everyone learn to communicate better?" She gave me a pointed look. "Maybe that's something for the group to discuss at our meeting next month."

Stammering, I said, "I'll see if there's a non-fiction book on the topic."

Gage stood and held up his coffee cup. "I'd like to toast this group of family, friends, and my future wife. The last couple of years has been filled with growth in our skills, making new friends who have become family, and expanding our hearts. Here's to us all, especially my favorite person in the world, Lily."

Mugs clinked, Brutus woofed, and Milo hopped onto my lap. "See, my dear witch, everything always works out as it should. But, of course, you would have known that if you kept reading your book."

"I love you, too, Milo." I kissed his head and plucked a healthy slice of smoked salmon from the bagel platter. "This is for you."

He took his treat and ran into the living room with Brutus on his tail. Life was sweet.

Sunday morning, the sun was high in the brilliant blue sky. Milo sat with me on the deck while I sipped coffee. Brutus lay close by, his tail thumping as if he knew today was special. I frowned when I took a sip of my now-cold coffee.

Milo said, "You know how to warm it up."

I wrapped my hands around the mug and closed my eyes. Soon, warmth radiated from the cup, and a small spiral of steam teased my nose. "I do love being a witch."

"Are you excited for today?"

"Yes, we need to get ready, but I wanted to take this moment to be with you. It's been just the two of us for a long time." I stroked the top of his head, down his back. "Thank you for being the best you." Tears sprang to my eyes, and I wasn't even sure why.

"My dear witch, none of that. You haven't read the book about fixing red eyes."

I laughed softly, wiped the dampness from my cheeks, and said, "You're right." I heard tires crunch in the driveway. "Quiet time is over, little man."

He hopped down and said, "Don't forget our bowties."

"Aunt Mimi's in charge of putting them on you and Brutus and securing the rings."

Nikki carried three garment bags up the steps. Mom and Glinda each carried boxes of flowers, and Aunt Mimi had the hat box. What's a beach wedding without a proper hat?

"Good morning." I stood up. "Am I running late?"

"Honey, the photographer will arrive in an hour, and we will take pictures here and then head to the town square for the ceremony. Regan and Fred Wickshire have everything under control for the reception, so there's nothing to worry about."

I pulled my robe close, and joy washed over me. "Then let's get ready."

A deep Southern voice drifted around the corner of the house, "Before you do, can I get a hug from the bride?"

Dax Peters sauntered up the stairs, and I ran to him, throwing my arms around his neck. He laughed and swung me in a circle. "Hello. If I'd known I'd get a greeting like that, I would have come earlier. Quite an ego boost for your old friend."

I slapped him on the arm. "You're family."

He put me down. "Gage asked me to give you this." He handed me a small box with a white bow. "Now that I've done my first duty as best man, I need to go find the old boy and make sure he's waiting for you at the altar."

I kissed his cheek. "Thank you, and tell Gage to look for the witch in white."

He laughed. "Consider it done." He smiled and gave a courtly nod. "Ladies."

I tore off the paper and nestled on black velvet was a diamond heart necklace intertwined with an infinity symbol. "Oh my stars, it's beautiful."

"He remembered." Glinda placed a hand on her heart. "This was my mother's necklace from my dad on their wedding day. I'm glad it's yours now."

I wanted my mom to put it on me, but it seemed right that Glinda should have that special honor. "Would you?" I held it out to her.

She looked at Mom, who nodded, tears brimming on her lashes. "Glinda, you do it."

I turned around as Glinda fastened it around my neck.

Aunt Mimi stepped forward. "There's powerful magic in your necklace. I can enhance it with your amulet; you'll have to wear one."

I nodded. "Yes, please."

My aunt stepped closer to me and held both pendants in her hands, closing her eyes. She lifted her face to the sky, and I wrapped my hands around hers. I felt a surge between us, and a moment later, she whispered, "And so it shall be."

I touched the diamond, and it pulsed under my fingertips. The families' power had merged. She kissed both cheeks. "Now it's time for you to step into your first gown. We don't want your groom to get overly anxious."

I held out my hand to my mother. "It's time."

Epilogue
Lily

I stood outside the Cozy Nook Bookstore with Dad. Nikki was gorgeous in her sage green dress, and she could transition from a long skirt to a short one for the beach reception. I smoothed my hand down the front of my gown; the sun caused the quartz crystals to sparkle like diamonds. The brim of my hat kept the sun from my eyes, so I wasn't squinting in the wedding photos.

"I hear music. That's our cue, Dad." I looked at the window seat inside the store. "Milo, Brutus, it's time."

Brutus trotted out, and I couldn't help but grin. His plaid bowtie matched the pale sage leaves on the wedding cake. Milo strutted into the sun, turning his head from side to side. "Is my tie straight?"

I reached down and made a slight adjustment. "It's perfect. You and Brutus can follow Nikki across the street."

He bowed his head. "Lily, you're a beautiful witch. Gage Erikson is lucky."

A lump rose in my throat. "Thank you, Milo." I gestured with my bouquet for him to start walking. "We need to go."

Dad hugged my arm to his body. "Milo's right, you're the most beautiful witch I've ever seen." He kissed my cheek. "I'm proud of all you've accomplished and look forward to what comes next for you and Gage."

"Thanks, Dad." I sniffed. "Let's go before I start blubbering and ruin my makeup."

He chuckled softly. "I know a spell to fix that."

I laughed. "Of course you do."

Gage

My heart stopped thumping in my chest the instant I saw Lily walk through the wrought iron gate into the town square. She seemed as if she was floating down the flower-strewn aisle. The chairs were filled with everyone from town, including council members and coven. At least, that's who Dax said they were. I noticed Laurel seated with other people from Pine Valley toward the back. Look at my favorite witch go, she's already bringing magicals and non-magicals together.

Dax's shoulder bumped me. "Breathe, my friend."

I flashed him a half smile that morphed into a wide grin. "Just look at her, isn't she beautiful?"

"You're a lucky man, that's for sure." He took a step back.

Reed smiled as I met them halfway. He shook my hand and placed ours together. "Be good to each other. Always treat the other the way you'd like to be treated, and Gage, welcome to the family."

"Thank you, sir."

She had my grandmother's necklace on, but there was something different about it. I'd have to ask her about that later.

Lily's smile was filled with a hint of mischief. "Are you ready for what comes next? The coven, family, and, of course, new puzzles?"

"I've been waiting my entire life for this day." I nodded to William, standing at the altar. "He's expecting us."

We walked hand in hand down the aisle, my eyes only for her. We stopped in front of William.

Milo and Brutus stood with Nikki and Dax.

William nodded to me and kissed Lily's cheek before whispering in her ear. She smiled.

"I'd like to thank everyone for joining Lily and Gage here today. This wedding has been a long-time coming. I promised my dear wife Lulu that when these two got married, I would get one of those one-day licenses to do the honor." He looked up at the deep blue sky, kissed the palm of his hand, and waved. "Here we are, my darling."

Clearing his throat, he grinned. "Gage, do you take Lily to be your companion in life for all your days on earth?"

"Yes. I do always and forever take Lily Michaels to be my partner in life."

"Lily, do you take this mere mortal to be your companion in life for all your days on earth?"

She grinned. "Yes, I do, and for all eternity."

William nodded. "In front of your family and friends, I pronounce you husband and wife."

Before he could say, *you may kiss your*

bride, I heard, "Welcome to the family, Detective Cutie."

I scooped Milo up and held him aloft. *Did you just say something?*

Milo placed his paw on my cheek. "Kiss your bride, DC, and make us an official family."

I handed him to Dax and wrapped my arms around Lily. Before our lips met, I said, "I can't wait for our life together."

Her eyes twinkled. "Kiss me."

I dipped her in my arms and kissed her.

Laughing, she said, "Now, let's go enjoy our bash at the beach."

Applause rang out, and confetti sprinkled down on us.

I looked up but didn't see a net. "How did that happen?"

She kissed me again and whispered, "Magic, my love."

"You are my favorite witch." I held her hand as we walked up the aisle.

If you loved Weddings & Wands, help other readers find this book:

Please leave a review now!

Are you ready to read more from the Lily and the gang in Pembroke?

Keep reading for a sneak peek at
Ghosts & Gowns
A Craft and Ghost Cozy Mystery
A Dress Designer Cozy Mystery Series
Order Now
Or
Shop at Lucinda Race

Lucinda

I hope you want to keep up with my crazy antics of writing, gardening, cooking, and life with the pups.

Not ready to stop reading yet? If you sign up for my newsletter at www.lucindarace.com/

newsletter, you will receive an excerpt for Cookies & Capers, the introduction of when Lily met Milo right away, as my thank-you gift for choosing to get my newsletter.

Ghosts & Gowns

Enjoy this humorous, small-town, psychic, cozy mystery by best-selling and award-winning Lucinda Race.

*S**he didn't want to talk to ghosts or investigate a murder.***

Designer and reluctant ghost whisperer Claudia Grant has moved to the picturesque small town of Drakes Bay to reopen her late uncle's dress shop. To her surprise, Uncle Herman didn't die of natural causes, and an even bigger surprise, his ghost has taken up residence in her shop.

On Claudia's first day in town, she meets Beth, a fellow shop owner. While cleaning fingerprint dust, Claudia receives a phone call from a local man claiming Herman planned to sell her shop to him. Curiosity piqued— she agrees to a meeting. The police burst in while she's hovering over his dead body, holding a gun.

As the only suspect and the real killer on the loose, Claudia must follow the clues linking these two murders. With some help from her new friends, including a handsome cop, can she figure out whodunit before the police slap on the handcuffs and formally charge her with murder?

If you enjoyed a Bookstore Cozy Mystery Series, this spin-off series should be on your TBR. Ghosts & Gowns is the first book in A Paranormal Ghost Cozy Mystery Series. It's a light-hearted, small-town psychic cozy mystery that guarantees the culprit is caught. Although each book can be read as a standalone, it is best to read them in order. Enjoy!

Visit Drakes Bay, the charming paranormal ghost series that is just a short drive from Pembroke Cove, Maine.

Ghosts & Gowns
A Craft and Ghost Cozy Mystery
Order Now

Social Media

Follow Me on Social Media

Like my Facebook page
Join Lucinda's Heart Racer's Reader Group on
Facebook
Twitter @lucindarace
Instagram @lucindaraceauthor
BookBub
Goodreads
Pinterest
YouTube

A Free Story for You

Have you enjoyed Weddings & Wands? Are you not ready to stop reading yet? If you sign up for my newsletter at www.lucindarace.com/newsletter, you will receive Cookies & Capers, the start of Lily and Milo's adventure, as my thank-you gift for choosing to receive my newsletter.

Cookies & Capers

I stood in front of the old wood and glass door as I pocketed the keys to the Cozy Nook

Bookshop. Aunt Mimi had signed her bookstore over to me. She said it felt like giving me her baby. But I loved the shop as much as my aunt did. We had worked together for the last twelve years. After attending the University of Maine, I had a degree in history and education. I had always wanted to be a teacher, but jobs were scarce and after substituting for a few years, I moved back to my hometown of Pembroke, Maine, and Aunt Mimi hired me as soon as I unpacked my suitcase.

Spending time with my aunt, learning the business, had been the best experience. I offered to buy the shop when she wanted to retire, but she wouldn't hear of it. As long as she had free books for life, and her long-term boyfriend Nate, she said it was a fair deal. From my point of view, I had built-in backup for years to come.

Now that I was the bookshop owner, Aunt Mimi was no longer coming in every day which meant her cat, Phoenix, wasn't either and the space felt empty without a kitty lying in the window or skulking about as kitties do. I was off to the Pembroke Animal Palace to see if I could find a match.

It was a short walk in the bright noonday sun. The spring air from the ocean carried a tang of salt, but the breeze was refreshing. I waved to one of my best friends, Gage Erikson, as he drove past in his police-issued sedan. My heart fluttered in my chest.

He was a detective on the force. Not that we had much crime in our small seaside town. But one of these days I was going to get brave and tell him I had been carrying a torch for him since we were in ninth grade. What's the worst thing that could happen? We'd still be best friends, right?

I continued down the brick sidewalk, waving to William North from the Sweet Spot Bakery. He was sweeping the area around the small bistro tables in front of the bakery. William was wearing a large pristine white apron and a wide smile. A deep inhale confirmed my suspicion. He was baking cookies.

My mouth watered. I did a half turn and went back to where he was finishing up. "Good morning, William." I bobbed my head in the shop's direction. "What is that tantalizing smell?"

He held open the brightly polished glass door. "One of your favorites, Lily. Chocolate chip and pecan cookies. Can I interest you in one before you continue on your mission?"

I gave him a side-look. "Mission?"

He chuckled. "Over the years my Lulu had said you had two speeds, strolling and purposeful. Just now, it was purposeful, so hence, you're on a mission."

"I'm going to the shelter, hoping to find a kitty. The shop is lonely now that Phoenix is home every day with Aunt Mimi, and I think a cat napping in the window adds an air of serenity to the place."

"Unless you're allergic."

He had a point, but I was not willing to be deterred. I smiled. "I'm always happy to deliver to a customer." I leaned over the glass bakery case, like a kid pressing her nose against the candy case. "You made sugar cookies too and frosted them?" I sighed. I was going to need to exercise more if he continued to bake all my favorites. He was smiling at me as I looked up. "Are the chocolate pecan ready?"

He wiggled his eyebrows. "I have a tray cooling in the back."

"Then can I have one of those and a sugar cookie, but to go?"

With a flick of his wrist, he snapped open a white bakery bag and called over his shoulder. "Jerilyn, would you please bring out the last batch of cookies?"

I heard a muffled, coming, and smiled. "It's good that Jerilyn stayed on." I said nothing about his beloved wife Lulu. Rumor had it she was ill and not doing well.

He nodded. "It is. She's a hard worker and excellent with the customers."

Jerilyn bustled in from the back room carrying a large stainless-steel tray. It was lined with parchment paper and cookies the size of the palm of my hand. It was going to taste so good with a hot cup of tea later.

William put two in the bag, along with two sugar cookies, and then he handed it to me. I paid for my cookies and thanked him. "Stop by the shop later. You might just get to meet my new fur baby."

"Sounds like a plan." He grinned and crossed his arms over his rounded midsection. "You're more like your aunt than you realize. Ever since she opened that bookshop, she's had a cat, too."

I paused, tucked the bakery bag in my tote, and with my hand on the door, I turned and gave him a wide grin. "And now it's time I carry on the tradition." With a jaunty wave, I called, "Wish me luck."

Cookies & Capers is only available by signing up for my newsletter – sign up for it here at www.lucindarace.com/newsletter

Love to read?

All ebooks and paperback copies can be ordered from my website at:

Shop at Lucinda Race

Cozy Mystery Books

A Bookstore Cozy Mystery Series

Books & Bribes

It was an ordinary day until the book of Practical Magic conked Lily on the head causing her to see stars. And then she discovered her cat, Milo, could talk.

Catnaps & Crimes

The fun continues as Lily practices her magic and needs to investigate another murder.

Tea & Trouble

A fall festival, reading tea leaves and a few clues propel Lily into a new murder investigation.

Scares & Dares

What goes wrong at a haunted house is anything but expected until Lily starts following the clues.

Holidays & Homicide

Can Lily solve a murder before it ruins the holidays?

Leprechauns & Larceny

Will a dead leprechaun take the shine off the wedding?

Magicians & Murder

When four magicians roll into town for a show more than fun is on one person's mind.

Artifacts & Amulets

Milo has been keeping secrets, which can be deadly.

Cranberries & Criminals

Whose half-baked idea was it for bookstore owner and witch Lily Michaels to enter an amateur baking contest in her small town of Pembroke Cove, Maine?

Broomsticks & Blooms

The time has come for Lily to learn to fly.

Fishing & Forgery April 2025

A simple Sunday fishing adventure with friends where Lily and her friends reel in the big one.

Wands & Weddings May 2025

Lily and Gage are ready to tie the knot. But what's up with the coven's council? Can Lily unravel this new mystery before she says, I do.

Ghostly Gowns Series

A Paranormal Ghost Cozy Mystery Series

Ghost and Gowns June 2025

Buttons & Burglary July 2025

Ribbons & Robbery August 2025

Witches of Robins Pointe

A Paranormal Cozy Mystery Series

Inherited Magic & Murder January 2026

Touch of Magic February 2026

Waiting for Magic March 2026

Cowboys of River Junction

Second Chances in Montana

Twenty years later, Renee and Hank are back where they fell in love, but reality is like a spring frost, and is a long-distance relationship their only option for their second chance?

Stars Over Montana

The cowboy broke her heart, but he never stopped loving her. Now, she's back ready to run her grandfather's ranch...

Hiding in Montana

Can love flourish while danger lurks in the shadows?

Moonlight Over Montana

From the smoldering ash, she realizes he's all the family she and her daughter need.

Standalone Titles

Shamrocks are a Girl's Best Friend

Will a bit of Irish luck and a matchmaking uncle give Kelly and Tric a chance to find love?

The Matchmaker and The Marine

She vowed never to love again. His career in the Marines crushed his ability to love. Can undeniable chemistry and a leap of faith overcome their past?

<u>Sundaes on Sunday</u>

A widowed school teacher and the airline pilot whose little girl is determined to bring her daddy and the lady from the ice cream shop together for a second chance at love.

Barrett

Has the last man standing finally met his match?

Marie

Career-focused city girl discovers small town charm can lead to love.

Price Family Romance Series

Breathe

Her dream come true may be the end of his...

Crush

The first time they met was fleeting; the second time restarted her heart.

Blush

He's always loved her but he left and now he's back... the question, does she still love him?

Vintage

He's an unexpected distraction, she gets his engine running...

Bouquet

Sweet second chances for a widow and the handsome billionaire...

A Holiday Romance

Holiday Heart Wishes

Heartfelt wishes and holiday kisses...

Holiday Heart Wishes

Hockey, holidays, and a slap shot to the heart.

Christmas in July

She's the hometown girl with the hometown advantage. Right?

<u>A Secret Santa Christmas</u>

Christmas just isn't Holly's thing, but will a family secret help her find the true meaning of Christmas?

The Sugar Plum Inn

The chef and the restaurant critic are about to come face to face.

Holiday Romance Box Set

Sweet with a touch of heat holiday romance novels.

The MacLellan Sisters Trilogy

Old and New

An enchanted heirloom wedding dress and a letter change three sisters' lives forever as they fulfill their grandmother's last request to try on the dress.

Borrowed

He's just a borrowed boyfriend. He might also be her true love.

Blue

Will an enchanted wedding dress work its magic one more time?

McKenna Family Romance Series

Lost and Found

Love never ends... A widow who talks to her late husband and her handsome single neighbor who has secretly loved her for years.

The Journey Home

Where do you go to heal your heart? You make the journey home...

The Last First Kiss

When life handed Kate lemons, she baked.

Ready to Soar

Kate will fight for love, won't she?

Love in the Looking Glass

Will Ellie's first love be her last or will she become a ghost like her father?

Magic in the Rain

Dani's plan of hiding in plain sight may not have been the best idea.

After All These Years

Arielle Clark is a famous artist with a painful past. When her first love comes to town, ghosts from the past are resurrected. But can the embers of love still linger after all these years?

About the Author

Award-winning and best-selling author Lucinda Race is an avid fan of fiction. As a young girl, she spent hours reading cozy mystery and romance novels, getting lost in the fun and hope they represented. While her friends dreamed of becoming doctors and engineers, she dreamed of becoming an expert at crafting captivating novels.

As life twisted and turned, she wrote nonfiction but longed to return to her true passion. After developing the storylines for the McKenna Family Romance series and the Paranormal Cozy Nook Bookstore Series, she decided to start living her dream. Her fingers practically fly over computer keys. She weaves paranormal cozy mystery stories and romance with guaranteed happily ever afters.

Lucinda lives with her two little dogs, a miniature long-haired dachshund and a shitzu mix rescue, in the rolling hills of western Massachusetts. When she's not immersed in her fictional worlds, writing mystery, suspense, and romance novels she's reading everything she can get her hands on.